"I'll give you one chance to get on your knees and beg me not to shoot you."

Tug figured maybe the bullet's punch would be quick and lethal and he'd never even feel it. Anyway, he told himself, he'd closed all the doors behind him. There was just one he must step through now. And maybe if he got lucky, he'd take this derby-wearing son of a bitch with him.

From in front of Dr. Salvador's Dentist Office, the town lawman, Trout Treadneedle, called out. "Hold up, boys!"

The man in the derby, the man who called himself the Mortician, jerked his eyes toward Trout.

"Stay the hell out of this, dad."

"I'm the law and if you don't disarm yourself—"

"You'll what?" the Mortician said, cutting off Trout's threat. He wasn't in any moods for threats. That wasn't how he operated. It wasn't how he ever operated.

Trout looked at Tug and the man in the derby and knew that now he was caught up in things. That was the problem about taking other folks' money to defend them, you couldn't just walk away and make believe their troubles weren't your own. . .

By Bill Brooks

The Journey of Jim Glass
THE HORSES
A BULLET FOR BILLY
RIDES A STRANGER

Dakota Lawman
THE BIG GUNDOWN
KILLING MR. SUNDAY
LAST STAND AT SWEET SORROW

Law for Hire
SAVING MASTERSON
DEFENDING CODY
PROTECTING HICKOK

BILL BROOKS

THE HORSES

HARPER

An Imprint of HarperCollins*Publishers*

HARPER

An Imprint of HarperCollins*Publishers*
10 East 53rd Street
New York, New York 10022-5299

Copyright © 2008 by Bill Brooks
ISBN: 978-0-06-088598-4

First Harper paperback printing: January 2008

HarperCollins® and Harper® are registered trademarks of HarperCollins Publishers.

Printed in the United States of America

Visit Harper paperbacks on the World Wide Web at www.harpercollins.com

10 9 8 7 6 5 4 3 2 1

For Joe Boschen,
who I've drank beer and
watched the river with.

THE
HORSES

Chapter One

A lone shadow moved through the cold rain. The horses stood silent in the corral, their ears pricked at the movement. Inside Jim and Luz slept side by side, dreamless, his arm around her, joined hip to hip.

The icy rain stung like needles. A bit colder and it would turn to snow. The dull sound of distant thunder rumbled like cannon in another valley. The shadowy figure had come from over the ridge, a long knife in one hand, the kind butchers use.

Jim turned once, opened his eyes to the dark room, then closed them again when he realized the woman was beside him.

The shadow moved past the gravestones atop the ridge, did not pause but descended toward the house, the corral, the nervous horses. The rain clattered off the metal roof of the house, and the wind swept along the porch like a cold broom. Farther north, higher up in the Capitans and even in the faraway Sangre de Christos it was snowing, several inches an hour. The time was the darkest hour before dawn.

The shadow had an off gait but moved steadily down toward the corral. Paused at one point, then moved again with the caution of a wise wolf.

Jim dreamed of horses. Wild horses. In his dream they ran free, their manes fluttering in the wind, their tails lifted out behind them. In the dream he had a rope that he could throw true, and gathered in the horses one by one. It was hot, steady work in the dream, and when he reached the river he and the wild horses drank, and they looked beautiful in the bright sun, their reflections floating in the water, and he was glad for their existence.

The shadow closed on the corral. The horses did not protest, sensing no danger, perhaps believing the shadow was the man from the house who came each day and fed and watered them. The rain tamped down any scent the horses might have had of the stranger. The rain boiled up around their hooves, slicked their hides dark and caused their muscles to ripple, and they didn't care for it much.

The shadow spoke softly to them, trying to calm them as he slipped between the cottonwood rails of the corral. There were six horses, not including the fine stud that roamed free in the far pasture, the one the man in the house had broke to a saddle and trained to come at his whistle. The stud could not be seen in the deep wet darkness, just the six gathered there in the corral.

The shadow came up to the first of them and reached forth the hand not holding the knife, and when the animal snuffled the small green apple the man held, the knife came up swift and sure and plunged into the jugular, then ripped quickly across the animal's neck, sending it instantly to its knees. An arc of blood thick as a rope hosed the air and splattered into the already wet ground as the horse kicked its legs in a struggle with death it could not outrace. The shadow had already moved on to the next animal before the first stopped kicking—a small sorrel—and let it snuffle the apple and repeated the murder, and yet again and again until all six horses were down, bled or bleeding out, dead or dying.

The shadow looked toward the house, his slicker smeared with blood, the cuffs of his shirt, his face and hands covered in it, the blade of the knife dripping with it, like red rain. He washed the blade in a puddle, then slipped back between the corral logs and started again toward the ridge, muttering low to himself as he went: "Now maybe you'll shut up. Now maybe you'll shut up."

Jim Glass slept as he dreamed of wild horses; the woman next to him hardly moved, her dark hair spread over the pillow. She did not dream but lay in a deep, black void of nothingness, the sweetest kind of sleep.

A sudden clap of thunder shook the whole house, and Jim awakened reaching for the handgun he kept beneath the bed—a Merwin Hulbert First Army Model Revolver. Its ivory grips were smooth and comforting. It was nickel-plated, a single-action .44-caliber, and he had killed men with it. It had its own history of death that went unspoken.

He gripped it as he listened. The rain troubled itself against the window glass, sounded like flung sand at times. He felt his pulse ticking in his wrists. Still he listened for any sound that shouldn't be there. And when he heard nothing more, he set the pistol back in its place and withdrew his hand and closed his eyes again.

The shadow climbed the ridge with difficulty; the lightning that produced the clap of thunder lit the entire ridge and the shadow in hot flashes, and at one point, if Jim had been looking, he could have plainly seen the shadow standing by the two gravestones before it disappeared over the far side just as the boom of thunder rattled the world.

To heaven's God, the horses in the corral looked as if they were sleeping on their sides. Six sleeping horses with stiff straight legs. The rain washed their bodies as if the horse gods were preparing them for some strange and final journey. Ministered to them the last cold balm of water upon their distended tongues and washed over their bared teeth and frightful glazed eyes.

The man in the house would not appear in the

morning to feed them, to look them over with a certain pride that the horse catcher has in his stock. And he would not take them into the nearby town and sell them as he'd planned. They were now forever free of ropes and saddles, bits and bridles and the spurs of men. Free of riding a man or woman or child on their backs. And no more either would they run free and wild upon the mesas and over the high desert.

Morning's first caustic light revealed the snows had come down from the Capitans and the Blood of Christ Mountains too, and mantled the land and dead animals in thin, sugary coats of white so that they seemed not made of flesh and blood and bone, but of crystal. And around them in the pocked earth of the corral were glazed red puddles and small crimson rivers that traversed the mud like bloody veins. Their once proud and beautiful manes were frozen in stiff bristles and strings, their tails matted to the frozen earth.

In the distance the stud horse that was the man's personal mount whinnied and trotted off, its gaze back toward the house, no doubt smelling the cold odor of death now that the winds had shifted round.

The smell of blood, like the smell of an apple, drew its curiosity.

Chapter Two

Jim woke to the bright morning light coming through the small, four-paned window in the back bedroom. Turned his face away from it, and when he did his lips brushed Luz's silken black hair. He reached out and touched one bare shoulder, and she stirred. Her skin was warm, even with the chill in the room. He rolled closer to her, and she reached back without opening her eyes and touched him.

"I think that storm's blown through," he said softly. It was now so quiet, they heard the house re-settling as the cold began to give way to the warmth of a rising sun that pressed its heat against the adobe walls and shake roof.

"Mmm . . ." she sighed.

He liked having her there in his bed. He thought she liked it too, because it had become a regular event over the past year since he'd first hired her to come once a week and clean his house.

Funny, how people went from being complete strangers to such deep intimacy without planning on it. And funny too, he thought now as he lay there close to her, the curve of her body fitting quite well the curve of his own, how he never thought it possible to be so deeply in love with any woman. Until Luz, he had always thought of himself as someone going it alone. Women, until her, had been temporary distractions in his life—nothing to be taken seriously, to be mulled over and wondered about beyond the bedroom door.

It wasn't to say he hadn't thought about it before it ever happened with her; he had, almost from the first time he saw her there working in the kitchen. Otherwise he would have never asked her to stay that one evening to have supper with him. But he never would have dreamed that a woman as aloof and almost stately in manner as Luz would ever find anything charming or likable in him. He'd led a restless and often hard life, had done things he wasn't proud of and things he'd never tell anyone about—some of them murderous things.

He'd had other women, lots, maybe more than his share. But he never loved any of them, though a few he thought he was in love with at the time, like the wife of the Nebraska rancher. No, these weren't the things a man talked about, especially to a woman like Luz.

"I best get up and go take care of my horses," he said.

She rolled over to face him, their noses a mere inch apart, their breath warm against each other's faces.

"Maybe you should take care of your woman first," she said with a smile.

"Maybe I should," he said. "Is that what you are now, my *woman*?"

"Yes, I think that is what I am."

"I like the sound of it, *my woman*."

"I do too."

He drew her against him until their flesh was pressed together, their bodies becoming as one, their legs and arms entwining, their mouths coming together in long, deep kisses. His blood rushed through him hot and eager, and she offered herself to him just as eagerly, it seemed, knew just how to accept him into her. It was, she thought, not so unlike the rituals of church, the ritual of communion, an offertory of flesh and desire, one to the other.

"Take of me," she whispered, "and I will take of you."

A struggle of passion, urgent, muscular, yielding, overcoming, rising and falling like strong ocean waves crashing upon the shore, bringing pleasure so deep it came near to the point of pain.

The sun continued its ascent, and its strength struck the newly fallen cap of snow a glancing blow. Water from the melting snow dripped from the eaves, and shrank where it lay upon rocks, leaving wet shadows on the gray stone from the sun's warm breath.

The day held the promise of new life. But the horses did not rise up from their deathbed. They did not whinny and cavort, calling to him to come feed them their portion of grain and oats mixed with honey. The mares did not whicker to the stud for attention. But the stud had come anyway, standing now at the fence line, its ears pricked, snuffling nervously.

An hour more passed as quickly as a minute in their wrestling pleasure until at last they fell apart like a broken thing and lay there breathing heavily.

Somewhere they could hear the trickle of water.

At last Jim rolled to the side of the bed and sat up.

"What's wrong?" she said.

"Nothing. I don't know. I've just got this strange feeling is all."

Her fingers traced the curve of his back, paused by the scars—three of them—small, oddly round, hard puckered. She knew what had caused them without asking. Her father and one brother had both been shot—not fatally—and had such scars as well.

He'd shown up in Domingo a little over a year ago and bought the Bowdre place—Charlie dead, Manuella gone off to live with relatives. She had known Manuella while Charlie was still alive. Had known Charlie too, a little. A quiet man with dark fierce eyes and heavy black mustaches that hid his mouth. She'd heard rumors about him: that he stole horses and cattle with Billy Bonney—the one they called "Kid"—and some others. Then Garrett got elected sheriff of the county and wiped them all out, Charlie and the Kid and the others. And when they brought Charlie's body to her, wrapped in a tarpaulin, Manuella simply went off, leaving the house abandoned until this stranger who was now Luz's lover arrived one day and bought the place.

He'd come into Domingo inquiring about a housekeeper. Octavio Ruiz, the barber, mentioned her name and he called on her. She had been hanging fresh-washed clothes to dry when he rode up and sat his big horse outside her fence. He spoke to her directly.

"I understand you hire to clean houses," he said.

"Yes."

"I could use the help."

She saw in him something she did not see in most men—something not so easy to describe, but something that gave her a sense about him that she could trust him, that he was a man of his word and did not give it loosely.

"Do you drink?"

"A little whiskey now and then, but nothing to worry about. I'm not a drunk if that's what you're concerned about."

He had an easy manner about him, leaned his weight on his forearms atop the horn of his saddle, never took his eyes from hers, and yet did not make her feel as though he were stripping her out of her clothes like some men would.

She agreed to his terms—three dollars each time she cleaned, once a week. It seemed fair considering it was a small house. He lived alone. She was surprised at how little she had to do the first time she arrived. Everything was neat and orderly, the dishes clean and stacked, the silverware put in a drawer, an oilcloth over the table. There was dust in the corners and under the bed and along the windowsills, cobwebs up in the corners of the ceiling and the windows needed a good washing. Nothing remarkably dirty or out of place for a single man. But what caught her eye was the shelf of books. She was drawn to them. So few people she knew were able to read, and fewer kept books in their house.

"Which is your favorite?" she said that first time, going over to the shelf.

"Shakespeare," he said.

She was ashamed that she herself could read very little, her name, her children's names, a few food labels on tin cans. Formal education had not been a priority of her parents.

"Borrow one if you like," he said.

She felt herself flushed with embarrassment, too proud to tell him she wasn't able to read. So she took one at random, the largest one, and said, "I'll borrow this one."

He came over just then and cocked his head, looking at the lettering, and said aloud, "Cervantes, Spanish, like yourself. Good choice."

"Yes," she said. "He is one of my favorites." She'd never heard of Cervantes.

From there, their relationship progressed from employer and employee to something more—slowly, inexorably, and they both sensed that it would. They found more and more in common with each visit. They talked as she worked. He would sit at the kitchen table and talk to her, ask her questions about herself. She told him she had two children, a boy and a girl, that she was a recent widow, that her husband had been killed in an accident. He brewed coffee, and they sat and talked and drank the coffee in between her efforts to clean.

"What did you think of *Don Quixote*?" he asked several weeks after she'd borrowed the big book.

"Who?" she said.

"The book you borrowed. What did you think of it?"

"I liked it," she said, the lie already bitter in her mouth.

"Which part did you like best?"

She flushed and shrugged, feeling deep embarrassment. It was a small lie. But still it was a lie, and she could find no reason to tell it. And now she must tell another lie to cover the first one.

"All of it, I guess . . ."

"I'd love to hear you read it to me—pieces of it," he said. "I think you have a nice voice." She said perhaps sometime she would, and let it go at that.

Then the next time, she came out of the house to find him sitting on the porch near dusk. She'd arrived later than usual that day because her daughter was sick, and after she'd arrived, they'd talked away almost the entire afternoon. He was sipping from a glass of whiskey and branch water.

"You want some?" he said. She hesitated, knowing that they were becoming more and more familiar with each other—that she was reluctant to feel anything toward a man because of Hector, her late husband, the love she still carried for him, thinking that if she began to care for another man, it would somehow be an act of being unfaithful.

He held forth the glass.

"I won't make it too strong," he said.

"Sure, why not?"

She didn't know why she felt so emboldened except she did not want him thinking of her as weak or fearful of him.

He went in and got her a glass and poured some of his whiskey into it, and added the branch water from a metal pitcher. She sipped as they sat watching the sun come closer to the ridge line where two gravestones stood. He had told her about his friends who were buried there. How they came to die. It was a very tragic story. She assumed he had killed the men who killed his friends. He did not say he had; she merely assumed it.

"I like the smell of a man's cigarette smoke," she said. It was a habit he'd recently taken up, he confessed. He didn't know why he had, "Other than it helps keep my hands busy." She watched him smoke.

"Would you like one of these too?"

She again boldly said, "Yes."

He started to make her a cigarette, but she stopped him and said, "No, show me how to do it." And so he did and she smoked it, and they watched the sun descend and sink slowly behind the ridge. Far, far out they saw the Capitans risen against the sky like jagged rock teeth. Farther north, they knew but could not see, rose the Blood of Christ Mountains— the Sangre de Christos.

It was the beginning of them, that evening of sipping whiskey and smoking together.

The next time she came, he asked her to stay to supper and he even had it prepared, a sort of stew of beef and potatoes and carrots in a heavy black Dutch oven. They took their meal out of doors. It was a tranquil summer night where the light stayed a long time, turning golden before devolving into dusty haze and ultimately into a purple darkness. The night air came down from the mountains so cool she had to put a shawl over her shoulders. The whiskey helped warm her blood. At home alone, she had practiced rolling cigarettes until she was skilled at it, and when he went to make one for himself, she took the makings and did it for him. He was impressed, and she was glad that he was impressed.

The next time she stayed for supper he said, "I have a surprise," and brought forth a large walnut box—it was a Regina music box that was labeled as having been made in Switzerland. He cranked the handle, and it began to play a waltz.

"Might I have this dance?" he said. She felt flush and eager. And when they danced in the yard, it didn't matter that he wasn't graceful as Hector had been. She liked his laughter, the fact that he was tall and broad through the shoulders and chest. She liked too that he took pride in his appearance and that he treated her as an equal, something Hector did not always do.

The evening sky was streaked a brilliant orange for the longest time in the dying of the day. They danced in the yard as the color drained away, the sky turning to gunmetal edged by growing darkness. It was the first time he kissed her.

It was the beginning of them as one, and they both knew it.

"Are you sure?" he said.

"Are you?"

"I think so."

"I think so too."

He asked if she wanted to spend the night.

"I should go, what will people think?"

"Whatever they want to," he said. "I'm sure they will anyway and that some are already talking about us."

He cranked the box again when it wound down, and they danced again in the ever encroaching darkness, the moths throwing themselves at the lamp's light behind the window glass of the house where Charlie Bowdre had once lived with Manuella in silent desperation.

Their new beginning continued well into the night and into the next morning just as it had now, this morning after the night of the big storm.

With happy eyes, she watched him dress, enamored with the ropy muscles of his arms and legs and wished they could have spent the entire day in bed together.

"I'm going to go care for the horses," he said again, hitching one gallus over his right shoulder, then the other.

"I will make us breakfast."

He took one last glance at her as she stood naked and brown from the bed, then went out into the cold crisp air and knew instantly why he had felt so troubled that morning as he looked toward the corral and saw all the horses down.

The stud whinnied as if it understood today's sorrow.

And the only word that passed his lips was: "Goddamn."

Chapter Three

"**W**here you been?" the Mortician said. He'd been awake since first light, sitting beneath the tarp they'd strung between two skinny poplars to keep the storm off them. It rained first, then the rain turned to snow before the storm blew itself out east of them.

"I went off somewhere," the half-wit brother said.

"I can see that, but where you been?"

The half-wit squatted by the little fire the Mortician had started, reached for the pot of coffee sitting on the embers. The Mortician saw the half-wit's horse was lathered, its head drooping. Rode hard, he thought, but where to and where from?

He saw blood on the half-wit's shirt cuffs when he reached for the coffeepot, his hands and wrists shooting out the end of his slicker, saw flecks of blood up around his hairline and the fat lobes of his ears. What'd this boy go and get himself into, all that blood?

"You kill somebody?"

The half-wit sipped his coffee in silence, steam rising from the tin cup like a small cloud. He blew on it with fat pursed lips, staring into the void of his own mind; they were still talking to him even though he'd told them to shut the hell up.

"Ardell?" the Mortician repeated. "You kill somebody?"

"Coffee's hot as a horseshoe."

"Fuck the coffee, I asked did you kill somebody?"

He was a big boy, as most half-wits seemed to be. All brawn, no brain. What they lacked in the thinking department, they made up for in size. Kid brother, that was the thing, otherwise he'd've left him on his own a long time ago. But the old lady pleaded with him to take the boy along with him. Coughing on her deathbed red blood into a soiled handkerchief with lace tatting.

"You can't just leave him on his own, Cicero," she implored. "Boy like Ardell will come to a tragic end left to his own devices. Somebody will murder him or else he'll do something they'll lock him in the crazy house for. I couldn't stand the thought . . ."

The old lady had raised them even after the old man had run off and left her nearly destitute. She had struggled mightily, taken in laundry, cleaning houses, and eventually selling the only thing she had left to sell, the only thing lonesome men would pay for, the boys' uncle Hatch included.

It started with her doing it occasional, then turned more regular. He and Ardell would watch her go off at night, return late into the darkness of predawn, watch as she wearily fixed them a spartan breakfast of salt pork and hard clabber biscuits, then go and flop in the bed and sleep till afternoon, when she'd rise and go out and try and make something grow in a small garden, but without much success. She'd been pretty once, but by the time she'd resorted to doing what she needed to to keep them all alive, she wasn't pretty anymore.

But something got wrong with her, something in her blood, from all those men maybe, and she became more erratic, cursing without cause, sudden loud outbursts and talking to herself there at the kitchen table.

One of the men was a physician who drank heavily and he diagnosed her as having syphilis, said it had gone to her brain. Said she wouldn't live much longer, that she'd die crazy as a coot. Said she'd also become a lunger and if the one thing didn't kill her, the other surely would.

"You want, I can give her something to put her out of her misery," this man told Cicero, who had not yet become known as the Mortician.

"You mean put her down like a damn dog?"

"It'd just be a shot of air into her bloodstream. She wouldn't feel anything."

"Christ Almighty."

"I know it's a hard decision, son, but you want to see her end up getting worse than she is, dying slow like this. Slow and awful?"

She had her lucid moments, but they grew fewer and further apart. Then toward the very end, she pleaded for Cicero to take care of his half-wit sibling, who at the age of seventeen was already a head taller and fifty pounds heavier than Cicero.

He saw a frightened and dispirited woman near her last.

"Promise," she said.

"I promise."

Making her that promise was like cutting the last thread that had tied her to the earth, tied her to the real world. After that she did not come back anymore but stayed crazy. The worst was the day she came into his room stark naked and tried to kiss him.

"Jesus, Mama!"

He pushed her away and ran to get the doctor.

"I tried to warn you," the old sot said.

"I want you to give her that shot."

"Put her down like a dog."

"Yes, you old bastard."

The doctor nodded calmly and got his bag and came out to the house. It was raining that night too. Rain and shattering thunder, just like this past evening when he'd awakened at one point to find Ardell's bedroll empty, his horse gone. He half hoped the boy had just decided to ride off and lose himself to the world. And yet . . .

The doctor said to them both, "This will just take a moment, it's best you wait out here," and went into the room where she lay muttering gibberish and picking at herself, her pillow stained with bloody phlegm.

"What's he gone do?" Ardell said. Even a half-wit instincts trouble when it is afoot.

"Nothing. Treat the old lady is all."

Ardell fidgeted and wrung his hands.

It seemed like the doctor was in there a long time with her, but finally he came out.

"She's at peace now," he said. "You can go in and say your good-byes now."

They went in together.

"Mama," Ardell said.

But she did not answer or move.

"What's wrong with her, Cicero?"

"She's dead."

The half-wit stared at the passive features of his maw, her eyes open, staring, as if in surprise and wonderment; the bubble of air the physician had injected into her veins caught and stopped her heart in mid-beat. Her jaw dropped open as surely as if she'd been poleaxed. The physician, drunk as he was, forgot to close her mouth, or her eyes.

For a very long time, Cicero Pie, elder son of
Louisa Hetheridge Pie, widow of old John Folsom
Pie, scalawag and boozehound, had wondered
what it was to kill a man. He thought, staring at
the old lady, it was time to find out. Went straight
to his room where he had a converted cap-and-ball
.36-caliber Navy Colt—the only thing the old man
left behind, probably because he was too drunk
and in too much of a hurry to skedaddle. It rested
in a drawer full of old socks needed mending heel
and toe; he took it, checked the loads, stepped out
into the yard, and discharged it into the back of the
physician's frock coat as he was stepping into his
quarter-top.

"There, you son of a bitch," he replied to the
dying man's question, Why?

Ardell wet his pants at the suddenness of it.

But quickly enough they buried the old lady and
the physician in separate graves, hard work as it
was to dig two and not one, Ardell doing most of
the digging with a pick and shovel while Cicero sat
atop a pile of freshly dug earth smoking cigarettes
and contemplating futures that he willed into existence. He saw the two of them riding wild, taking
whatever they needed from the weak, drinking and
fucking whores, and nobody to tell them what to do
anymore. If it lasted a week, fine by him. If it lasted
a hundred years, better still. Killing, he thought, sitting there as the half-wit dug the graves, was about
as simple a thing as a man could do.

He said, "Before you drop that old fool into the hole, check through his pockets for money, a pocket watch. Most them carry a pocket watch."

After the corpses were planted, the two brothers ate the last can of beans and the last can of peaches in the house, then went to sleep in their beds.

Arising at first light, Cicero set fire to the homestead, and he and Ardell rode away in the quarter-top, their saddle horses tied to the back. They'd ride to the nearest town the opposite direction the one Doc was from, and sell the rig and pocket the money.

"I'd know how easy this shit was, being a outlaw," Cicero joked, "we'd a set out in the outlaw business a long time ago." Ardell still wondered why their maw had died so suddenly and why his elder brother had shot the doctor.

Cicero watched the half-wit blowing and sipping his coffee and thinking he had become as mysterious as death itself.

"How'd you get all that blood on you?"

Ardell looked down at his cuffs, rubbed the side of his face.

"Snow's purty, ain't it?" he said, looking at the thin blanket of freshly fallen snow, glowing, it seemed, even in that early light.

Cicero pulled on his boots thinking about those last two he'd killed—the bachelors owned them that sheep camp up in that valley north of where they were now.

How those two old men stood there gawking at Ardell, saying, "What's wrong with that boy?"

"Oh, ain't nothing wrong with him, he's just a little slow."

"By gar!" one of them declared.

They invited them to a dinner of mutton stew, them funny accents they spoke with, saying how they were originally from a place called Galway. How they came to America to make their fortune.

"This is cow country mostly," Cicero saying.

"Yes, we know."

Ardell imitating the bleat of sheep: "Bah, bah, bah . . ."

Again they wondered what was wrong with him, and Cicero showed them there wasn't nothing wrong with him by shooting them both at a distance the span of a kitchen table; so close it set their worn coveralls afire, Cicero putting the flames out with the rest of what was in the stew pot.

"There you sons a bitches . . . what is wrong with you?"

Ardell sitting there with the spoon halfway to his mouth, staring.

A year earlier Cicero had shot two lawmen in Las Vegas, New Mexico, who were going to arrest him and Ardell for loitering. They weren't expecting it, but they should have been. They were victims nineteen and twenty in Cicero and Ardell's year-long journey since having murdered the physician.

The *Las Vegas Optic* wrote that the killings were *heinous* and *depraved*, and the responsible party was, in the editor's opinion "... *a dealer in death not unlike a skillful mortician* ..." Several other lawmen appeared on the scene and arrested the brothers and a trial was held, but Cicero was acquitted of homicide by determination that the shooting was self-defense. The fact that Cicero testified the lawman had abused his half-wit brother and threatened to kill him on the spot.

Hence he earned for himself an odd and chilling nickname—the Mortician—thanks to a yellow journalist wag.

"I said where'd you get all that blood on you?" Cicero repeated when Ardell did not answer.

"Horses," he said.

"Horses?"

Ardell nodded.

"They kept talking and talking and talking to me," he said after several more moments of silence as Cicero moved to the fire and squatted across from the half-wit.

"What were they talking to you about?"

"They was saying bad things to me, things about maw," he said.

"Goddamn ..." muttered Cicero.

"I went and found them and killed them. Made them shut up!"

Cicero saw the big butcher knife the half-wit carried. He was not to be trusted with a gun.

"Well good on you," Cicero said, for he did not know what else to say.

Ardell continued to nod. His hip, the one he'd fallen off a roof and cracked just before the old lady died, gnawed at him when it got cold damp weather. Cicero saw how he limped when he stood and walked off toward the bushes and made water, worse than usual.

Horses! Cicero thought. *Fucken boy has lost the last of whatever sense he may have had. Dumber than a turnip, for sure.*

Ardell made yellow circles in the snow that seemed to delight him.

"Look," he said. "Look."

Chapter Four

He crossed the snow-laced ground to the corral but he already knew before he got there the horses were all dead. The frozen ground was pocked with bloody frozen pools. The horses lay staring, one eye pointed skyward, glazed from death and the cold. He stopped just there at the rails, the sun not yet risen high enough to have any warmth to it. He blew into his hands. His heart hammered steady inside his shirt, skin, muscle. He'd never seen anything like it. Six horses with cut throats.

His eyes lifted from the corpses to the land beyond what he owned until they saw the stud standing at the fence line, stock-still watching him. He whistled, and it whinnied and pawed the ground. He figured the reason it too had not been slain was that he'd had enough sense not to fence it in. A horse like that you don't fence in.

He crawled in between the rails and examined the animals closer, the way they'd been killed, and wondered about the stealth of whoever had done it. Even if any of them had raised a ruckus, he'd not heard it because of the storm. Whoever did this knew all there was to know about slaughter. It would have taken a big knife, sharp as a razor, and a good amount of strength and skill. Blood was frozen on the inside of the rails and posts, frozen in ropy red streaks that trailed downward like something a little kid with a paintbrush might do.

He stood after squatting next to the last of them—Luz's little sorrel filly with the four white stockings. She would grieve to learn of it, he was sure. He turned and eased out between the rails and crossed over to the house, his hands clenched into fists, his boots leaving a second set of tracks in the fresh snow—a trudge that spoke of loneliness.

Luz was there at the stove when he came in, fixing batter for flapjacks. She had pieces of ham frying in a pan and coffee brewing on the stove lid. The smells were warm and inviting and deceptively all wrong for what he was feeling. She'd set two plates on the table, a fork and knife and spoon for each.

She turned her head when he came into the mudroom, stomping snow off his boots. Saw the look on his face.

"What is it?" she said.

"I don't want you to go outside this morning."

"Don't be silly."

"I need to ride into town but I want you to stay inside the house."

"Tell me what's wrong."

"Somebody's killed the horses," he said, and went on into the bedroom and bent down under the bed and got the pistol, then reached into a cedar-lined closet to the top shelf and found the shoulder holster, and took it down and slipped into it and put the pistol into the holster, then put his coat on before coming back into the kitchen.

She was standing there unmoving, wondering if she'd heard him right, had tried looking out the window above the dry sink but could not see the corral from that view.

"My little Jessie too?" she said.

"Yes. If you have to go to the privy, go now," he said. "Otherwise I need you to stay put in this house till I get back."

He went to the corner of the room where the L. C. Whitney ten-gauge stood dark and lethal, all wood and steel, foreboding. Took it and broke it open and saw both chambers were seated with shells, then snapped it shut and set it in place again.

"I'll walk out with you to the privy," he said.

She went in and shrugged out of her nightgown and dressed in a pair of trousers and one of his flannel shirts, then laced up her shoes and came out into the kitchen again looking perfectly androgynous, especially when she put on one of his old canvas coats. They went out through the mudroom and walked the now hidden footpath to the privy, where he stood guard until she came out again. His eyes scanned the ridge and in every direction out away from the house. There was no good place a man could be lying in wait. He walked her back to the house.

"I'm going to ride into Domingo and talk to Trout," he said. "Do you feel safe waiting here alone until I get back? I can travel much faster if we're not riding double. You know well how to use that." He nodded toward the shotgun. "You don't have to be a shootist to hit anything with it; it will stop about anything, including something the size of a circus elephant. You just have to have enough grit to pull the triggers."

"Yes," she said, looking at it.

He had long before this moment taught her to shoot pistol, rifle, and shotgun. It was the kind of country a body needed to have such skills—man and woman alike. She didn't like the guns, the shotgun especially because it had a wrist-breaking kick to it, but she'd hit most of the cans and bottles he'd lined up for her. Good enough that he was satisfied she could defend herself, it came to that.

He took his Stetson from the wood peg and settled it on his head.

"Remember," he said, reaching for the door latch. "Nobody comes in you don't know, and if they try, give them both barrels. He reached onto a shelf and took down a box of shells with brass bottoms and red paper the size of a man's thumb. "I'll be back here in an hour."

The terrain was one of gently rolling hills, covered now with a thin blanket of snow so that the green of junipers stood dark against the white, so that the blue of sky seemed made of perfect blue glass, so that the Rio Ruidoso's water looked like a fat black snake crawling its way along. And where the sun struck the snow, it sparkled like broken glass.

And when he looked back at the house, he could see a curl of smoke from the tin smokestack knowing that she wasn't defenseless, that she was full of grit and seasoned, and for that he was well pleased. Still, the thought of what had been done in the night troubled him. And what troubled him even more was the why of it.

He spurred the big stud to a gallop for the trip to Domingo. The air brushed cold against his face and bucked inside his clothes. By midmorning the sun would gain enough strength to melt the snow except in the deepest shadows. Spring in this country was always chancy.

He kept an eye for any sort of movement, but saw none.

Except for the thudding hooves, the jingle of bit, the horse's breathing, the creak of cold saddle leather, the world was as silent around him as if he had been encapsulated in one of those children's glass domes.

The road was for the most part straight, but rising and falling over the gently sloping landscape, and thus far so early in the day, unscarred by wagon or horse tracks. He ascended a rise and descended the other side before fording a black creek that branched off the Ruidoso. Every little while he would turn slightly to check his back trail, thinking someone was following him. But he never saw anyone.

The previous night and this early morning's pleasure were all but forgotten now, replaced by the sight of something unspeakable.

It seemed as if a knot had been tied in his guts even as he made plans for his return—what he knew needed doing to keep the coyotes and buzzards and wolves from coming, to rid the place of the stink of putrefaction. Death could not stay no matter how onerous or tragic. Death had to be taken away and gotten rid of.

Soon he saw the dark outline of the town risen out of the new snow. He felt the anger in him building and knew he must keep it tamped down. There would always be more horses, he told himself. But that didn't mean whoever wanted to could simply violate him and his property.

He'd been trespassed against.

It was not a thing he could simply abide by.

He drew rein in front of the Cat's Paw Saloon. Inside he would surely find at this hour the man he was looking for—the town's constable, Trout Threadneedle, and the only real law there was in the area.

And by the time he walked through the double doors, he knew he was losing his battle with the anger inside him.

Chapter Five

He found the lawman sitting at the end of the bar in the Cat's Paw Saloon. There was a DeWitt's ten-cent romance and a cup of steaming coffee on the bar top before him.

Trout Threadneedle had hair like a woman, long and curly, the color of ashes, same as his flowing mustaches. Bilk, the saloon's owner, stood behind the bar across from Trout, sipping from a small glass of emerald green absinthe. Bilk's pinky ring winked in the light cutting through the window and spreading itself over the dark oak. The bar ran north to south along the east wall. An old upright piano stood along the opposite wall, as forlorn this time of morning as a man waiting in the rain for a train. Along the back wall was a big potbelly stove men would gather round in the winter. The tin ceiling was stamped into the shape of diamonds with

a fleur-de-lis in the center of each. Gaslights lined
the walls for when darkness fell too heavily into the
room. There were four tables, each with four chairs
men could sit and drink and play poker at, and a
wheel of chance stood waiting just where a hallway
began that led to two rear rooms, each with a single
bed—one for Bilk and one for the whore. At the
extreme rear was a small storage room where Bilk
kept extra barrels of liquor, and a back door kept
locked with a steel bolt.

"I got a problem at my place," Jim said, approach-
ing the lawman with due caution.

"What sort of problem?"

Trout's reputation was such that the truth was
all mixed up with the rumors until even he did not
always know for certain the veracity of his own
history. Among the rumors was a reputation for
shooting first and asking questions later. Supposedly
he had killed a fair share of men and done this and
that—teamster; gold miner; shotgun guard for the
Butterfield Stage Lines; deputy in Olathe, Kansas;
buffalo hunter in Texas; gambler and pimp in
Colorado. In other words, the normal life of an itin-
erant man of his day.

He was bulked out now, unlike the skinny man in
the photograph he carried in his shirt pocket—one
of him standing with one foot on a dead buffalo
holding a Sharp's Big Fifty from his Fort Griffin
days. All that thinness and youth were as long

gone as the buffalo now. His belly sagged over his belt buckle. He was nearly forty years old, and nobody had to tell him his string was running out. He figured his only shot at a future was to find a wealthy widow with property he could settle on to. But, ho! Show me a widow, he'd say to Bilk when the subject came round, and I'll show you a man willing to kill her other suitors just so he can plop every night in a feather bed and keep her well happy.

Trout was, however, in love with Little Paris, the town's only whore, who worked the suckers, ranch hands, any old boot who walked through the doors with a lonely heart and more than five dollars in his pocket he was willing to spend for fifteen minutes of dirty pleasure. Bilk was also in love with her. It was a touchy point between the two men and kept their relationship tentative and often taut as new strung wire.

"Horses all killed last night during the storm," Jim said.

"Horses killed?"

The look Trout offered up was one of incredulity. He'd never heard of such an event.

"What killed them?"

"Somebody with a knife. Slit their throats, bled them out."

Bilk whistled between the gap in his front teeth. He'd been thinking about Little Paris, who was back there now sleeping late as usual. She wouldn't get up till noon, then would want breakfast, her eyes all red from the cocaine pills, her words slurred, barely wearing anything at all. Him or Trout or any other man who looked at her could see the dark coins of her breasts through the thin cotton shift she wore. It displeased him to know his weren't the only eyes that beheld her tawdry beauty. Displeased him even more to know Trout had shared her pleasures and he hadn't, even though the Cat's Paw was his place of business and she kept her bed there and used it to ply her trade out of. He could have shared her pleasures too, but he was too proud a man to pay her for them. In his way of thinking, he wanted to win her love, and thought someday he might if he was just patient enough. Sooner or later, she'd realize wasn't no rich cowboy going to come and save her from the life—and that he, Bilk, was a steady and astute businessman, even if not wealthy.

"The hell you say," Trout replied, lifting his coffee to his mouth so that the steam gathered in his mustaches.

"I'd like your help finding the son of a bitch."

"I ain't no tracker if that's what you're thinking."

"Asking you to back my play when I catch up to him, if there's more than one. Besides, if I have to kill whoever it was, I want it to be legal."

"Hell, you'll get no grief from me, if that's what you're worried about. A man has a right to protect his own . . ."

Trout knew the reputation of the man facing him better than he knew his own: Jim Glass, former Texas Ranger, had himself been rumored to have killed out of revenge as well as duty several men, including a wealthy rancher—something over a woman, he thought it was. But you didn't need to know anything about what was in a man's past to gauge him: you could tell it in his eyes, the way he spoke and stood, his whole demeanor. Trout had encountered such men before, in Kansas and Texas and Colorado. Men who had that same unflinching look in the face of the worst kind of trouble. Cool as the inside of a cave. Men who didn't spend a lot of time arguing their case or debating disputes. They said what they had to say, then if that didn't untie the knot, they shot you. He himself was quick on the trigger and understood why a man needed to be. Hickok was that way, and so were Clay Allison and John Wesley Hardin. All of whom Trout had encountered along the way. Deadly men if you crossed them, and even sometimes when you didn't. Allison supposedly shot a man for snoring.

"I'm sort of tethered to this here town," Trout said, his upturned high-crowned Stetson resting on the bar stool next to him like a collection can. "I mean you live out there to the old Bowdre place which is clean out of town. I get paid by the citizens' tax money."

"I pay taxes too."

"Yes sir, that is a fat fact. Only your taxes are collected by the county sheriff, sure enough."

"You suggesting I ride a hundred miles or more to try and find him?"

"No sir, just saying what is fact is all . . ."

"You going to get off your fat rump or not?"

"Well, there ain't no need for insults. I'll come along and have a look."

Jim headed for the door. Trout traded miserable looks with Bilk. Trout had been reading aloud from the novel for benefit of Bilk, who was himself as illiterate as a three-year-old. The bargain between them was simple and straightforward: in exchange for Trout reading aloud the romances, Bilk would supply free meals and drinks. It was to Bilk's chagrin as much as it was to Trout's that he'd been suddenly summoned away smack in the middle of one of the more exciting parts of the romance—where Jack Long had just shot the panther in the eye.

"I shall return," Trout said with the unnecessary dramatic flair of a second-rate stage actor.

"I'll keep the coffee hot."

"Tell Little Paris when she gets up from her beauty rest I'll be by to have a turn with her."

Bilk frowned at the notion and thought: *You son of a bitch.*

Jim was already mounted on the stud awaiting Trout's exit from the saloon. The sun indeed had risen and gained strength enough to cause the snow on roofs to begin melting, the water dripping off eaves like tears. The broad avenue being churned into a muddy mire now that the town's traffic had begun—wagons and horse riders and pedestrians.

Trout rode a big bay that had U.S. stamped on its right flank. He walked it round parallel to the boardwalk so he wouldn't have to step up so far to get his bulk into the saddle.

"Say, I have an idea," Trout said, shifting his weight to gain balance on the cold hard leather seat.

"I'm listening."

"Know a half-breed Mex Apache who is a good tracker, not far north of here. You want somebody to track for you, he'd be your man."

"I don't want to waste a lot of time on this. I left my woman home alone. That son of a bitch comes back, who knows what might happen."

"Twenty minutes' ride is all it is to old Hairy Legs's place. We could cut cross-country from there, go through Sandy Pass to your place. Be the same amount of time, all told."

"Lead on, then."

Trout thinking in utter disquietude, *I wished I was laid up with Little Paris in her bed, or married to some land-owning widow so I could give up all this inconvenience. Marry the one, romance the other. A wife and a paramour, like those Frenchmen did it.*

The notion settled in him, like a piece of sweet candy.

Chapter Six

Ardell whistled through his teeth, thinking he had the ability to talk to birds, believing they talked to him. He whistled sharp and fluttery, trying to imitate any birds he heard that hid themselves in the poplars and cottonwood branches. He even tried to caw like a crow when he'd see one. And in the evening, he'd coo like Gambel quail or screech like a Harris hawk.

"What the fuck you do that for?" Cicero said. "Ain't you got no sense?"

"Talking to the birds."

"Yeah, what they telling you, that you're dumb as a ox?" Cicero was derisive in his comment. He could say about anything to that knothead brother of his and he'd not get its meaning.

"Telling me their secrets."

"What secrets is that?"

"Where they live, what it's like where they live, what it's like to fly."

"Lord God."

"Where we going?"

"Somewhere."

"I'm hungry."

"You just ate a pan of biscuits."

"I'm still hungry."

"Fine, we'll stop the next town we come to."

"I could eat a whole cow."

"I don't doubt you could."

"I wished I was married."

"I wished you was married too."

"I'd like me a wife and a screen door to keep the flies outta the house and a big long porch to sit on."

The boy's thinking was as jumbled as a jigsaw puzzle spilled from a box.

They rode along until they saw in the distance a small house with smoke curling out its chimney.

"Maybe we can stop there and get something to eat," Cicero suggested.

"Nah, nah, nah . . ."

"Why not?"

"I ain't going."

"Why not?"

"I just ain't."

"I thought you said you was hungry."

"I ain't going."

Cicero drew rein and looked at the half-wit. Then he looked off toward the house.

It was just a small house that had a porch on the front, a corral, a shed, and an outhouse, some fencing. Not far off he could see the arch of a river cutting through the hills and beyond the house a ridge, but that was all.

"What's got you spooked?"

"Nothing."

"You're acting like a mule with sore feet."

"Nothing."

"You ain't hungry now, is that it?"

The half-wit shook his head violently. He didn't want to say what he knew about that place—how the horses had talked and talked and talked to him, had called him.

"Well, we should ride down there and see what the score is. Sometimes opportunity knocks when you least expect it. Might be whoever lives there has got some money kept in a coffee can, some guns and horses we could take."

The mere mention of horses sent the half-wit into near spasms. He shook his head again, harder.

"Nah, nah, nah . . ."

Then he kicked his heels into the ribs of his horse and galloped off down the road in the direction they'd been riding.

Cicero looked again longingly at the house, thinking of possible opportunity, money kept in coffee cans, guns, horses, maybe a hot, home-cooked breakfast cooked by a fine-looking woman, and if she had a husband so what? He could make her a widow right quick, tell her when he done it, "The Mortician was here." See the look on her face. Him standing there all in black like death itself, his belly full of her breakfast, his desire all spent, that coffee can money stuffed in his pocket. He was as hungry for a woman as the half-wit was for food—woman and violence.

But shit, that half-wit Ardell was going to go and get himself lost or get into some sort of trouble. It was worse than watching after a two-year-old. One last quick glance toward the house before he spurred his horse.

Could be, too, there is some old coot living down there easily spooked and shoot me out of this saddle, he told himself to justify the decision to go on after Ardell instead of riding down to the house. *If wishes were fishes,* and he rode after the half-wit calling, "Hold up, you knothead."

It looked all around like a pretty day with the snow shriveling under the sun's heat and a warm southern breeze blowing up from the river. It could have been made more pleasant were it not for the half-wit's spookiness.

Maybe an accident will befall that boy, Cicero thought. *I mean what could I do about it if it did?*

Chapter Seven

They rode north at a good pace until they spotted a dugout resting along the high bank of the Pecos near the confluence of the Rio Hondo.

"That's him there, fishing," Trout said.

A lone figure sat under a large straw hat, a cane pole in his hand, the line dipping into the current.

The breed looked up sleepy-eyed at their approach, like an old turtle blinking in wonderment from beneath the brim of his sombrero.

"He claims he used to be a fierce warrior in his day, but look at him now, nothing but a sot who has to resort to catching mudcats out of the river to feed himself. But he's the best goddamn tracker I know of around these parts."

Trout reined his horse to a stop just there by the water's edge, and Jim sat alongside him.

"He can be an obstinate old bastard," Trout said, looking down at the breed.

Hairy Legs was dressed in a dirty blue cavalry jacket punctured with what looked like several bullet holes. Half the brass buttons were missing, and there were sergeant's chevrons on only one sleeve. He wore baggy wrinkled trousers made of canvas and patched with pieces of flour sack, the trouser legs several inches short of the tops of scarred brogans. His flesh was as brown and wrinkled as a walnut. But Jim could see the man had one brown eye and one blue. He didn't fail to notice, either, a fair-size butcher knife tucked in the red sash tied round his waist.

"That's a big knife," Jim said to Trout.

"Hell of a big knife. You thinking he done it, killed your horses?"

"Why don't we ask him."

Trout spoke to the Indian in a mixture of Spanish and Apache with some hand signals thrown in. Spoke in exaggerated tones, his voice overly loud.

Hairy Legs looked from Trout to Jim, both of them still mounted as he remained seated on the grassy bank, somber, his fish tugging the placid flowing river. But when it flooded during the winter and spring months, the river's personality changed to fury, a boil of tumbling, turbulent water force that had the power to wash away trees, houses, cattle, horses, humans, and even graves. One of the Pecos's more notable victims had been the house of Pete Maxwell in Fort Sumner, in whose bedroom Garrett had fed the Kid a bullet for supper. They buried the Kid and his pals—including Charlie Bowdre whose house Jim now owned—in the military graveyard in Fort Sumner. Some claimed the river's flooding had swept Billy and Charlie's bodies away, along with many others. A man in Las Cruces claimed to have the Kid's trigger finger in a jar, and a medicine show claimed to own the rest of the young killer's skeleton. What was true and what wasn't was left for conjecture. In this country, Jim knew anything was possible.

Hairy Legs had two fat carp on a stringer floating belly-up in the lazy current. His luck had obviously been good this day. Two fat fish for his supper would taste real good smoked over a fire.

"I asked him did he get drunk and kill some horses last night," Trout said after his first sharp and quick parley with the breed. "He said he didn't. Said he'd never kill a horse because horses were the brothers to the wind."

"You think he'd confess if he had done it?"

"No, I don't trust Indians no farther than I can throw a piano, having encountered my share along life's travails. And this one is part Apache—the worst sort of Indian. Add in that hot Mex blood and you don't know what you get, but whatever it is, can't be purty."

Then Trout engaged the breed again, who in turn shook his head and uttered a grunt of something.

Trout repeated whatever he said a second time, and finally the breed took out his knife and handed it up to Trout, who tested the edge with the ball of his thumb.

"He could have done it with this," Trout said. "You want to just go ahead and shoot him in the nuts or something? Because I don't reckon we're going to know the truth even if I arrest him and have him stand trial. You know those white people and those Mexican people who will sit on a jury, aren't none of them sympathetic to a breed. To the Mexes, he's Apache and to the whites, he's either one. Whatever the truth, he'll be found guilty whether he did it or not, but then what? Unless you want to see him hanged over it—killing your horses, I mean?"

The breed's long hair was full of stickers and burrs and pieces of grass, no doubt from having slept on the ground, and he looked ragged and worn out besides being half drunk. His wrinkled old face held the history of his life: defeated and beaten down at every turn—forced to catch trash fish instead of hunting game, his soul stolen by liquor, like what remained in the bottle by his right leg there in the grass.

Jim let himself venture a private guess: *Maybe if he had killed my horses, he probably thought of it as some small way of getting even with a white man for whatever misfortune he has suffered at the hands of white men.* But still, that blue eye—now that was something to behold, spoke of white blood, or high Spanish blood. Somewhere in this old man's heritage was more than just bad blood.

"Ask him what he thinks of white men?" Jim said.

Trout looked at Jim as though he was the biggest fool he'd ever seen.

"Ask him," Jim repeated.

Trout spoke even more forcefully and motioned with his hands pointing toward him and Jim.

The breed turned his gaze toward Jim and let it rest there for a long hard moment, then smiled and spoke something guttural again before turning his attention back to the river.

"What did he say?"

"He said white men fell from the sky like hard rain and drowned the Indians the same way they stole Texas from the Mexicans—that there was nothing the Apache or the Mexes could do about it because the whites came with such force. He said the white man is a plague to anyone who ain't white. I asked him if he would help track whoever killed your horses. He said he was too busy and had to catch three more fish. I'd say he's guilty as sin."

"Ask him who gave him that blue eye."

"He won't tell you."

"Ask him."

Trout did the asking and the old man simply ignored the question.

"Let's go," Jim said.

"You don't want to shoot him in the nuts?"

"He didn't do it."

"How can you be so sure?"

"Whoever did it was strong, powerful; he don't look like he weighs more than a hundred pounds if you put rocks in his pockets."

Trout sighed and turned his horse around after Jim turned his around, and they rode southwest cross-country to Jim's place, cutting up through Sandy Pass to save time. Within a mile of getting there, Trout said, "I do believe I smell chicken frying."

Jim sniffed the air but he didn't smell anything.

"You're invited to stay to dinner. That is if you don't already have a more pressing engagement."

"No, sir. I sure don't."

"First things first," Jim said as they neared the corral. "Around here a man has to work for his meal."

"I got a bad backbone."

Jim rode over, leaned and opened the corral gate, the double strand of wire looped to hold it shut.

Trout saw the miserable sight of six dead horses and spat his disgust, saying: "Jesus what is wrong with people?"

"We got to rope and drag these horses out away from the house," he said. Trout looked crestfallen. All he could think of was a hearty meal of fried chicken, maybe some gravy and biscuits to go along with it. And after dinner, a nice little snooze in the shade of some mimosa tree if he could find one.

The lawman followed Jim's lead and loosed his rope from where it hung on his saddle. He and Jim roped the dead horses by the hind feet acting as a team, and dragged them off to an arroyo a mile from the house and dropped them in. It was mean work no matter how they thought about it, but there wasn't anything more to be done about it other than do it.

By the time they finished, Trout's belly was growling with hunger in spite of the ghastly chore.

He followed Jim's suit in dismounting, and they washed their faces and hands in the cold ground-water pumped up by jerking up and down on the red pump handle there just outside the house, then wiped themselves dry on a hand towel hanging from a loop of wire wound round the pump head.

"That's the sorriest work I ever done," Trout said.

They went inside and sat around the table and ate fried chicken and candied yams and roasted ears of corn, washing it down with black coffee. No biscuits, no gravy, much to Trout's disappointment. Mostly Jim and Luz watched Trout eat like he didn't have no bottom to him. Five ears of corn and most of the chicken and yams.

"Jesus and Mary," Trout said when he gnawed the last of the chicken meat off a drumstick and wiped his fingers and swallowed the last of his coffee. "But I do believe I've never et anything that tasty in my whole life."

Luz forced herself to smile. She wondered if Trout's skinny whore ever cooked him a meal and doubted she ever did.

Then they all took their leave out on the porch where Jim poured each a short glass of whiskey and Luz rolled them cigarettes, Trout declining, saying he never had took up the habit because he couldn't see no sense in spending good money on tobacco just to roll it up in paper and smoke it. Jim and Luz smoked as low white clouds gathered over the Capitans like a shroud of sorrow.

"Whoever done this thing," Trout said, "more or less put you out of business, didn't they?"

Jim nodded.

"Least for now they have."

"I still think it could have been old Hairy Legs who did it. That knife of his is big enough to saw off a man's leg."

Luz said she knew of the breed, had seen him around Domingo.

"He's just an old man," she said. "Why would he do a thing like that?"

"Who's to say what goes on in a breed's mind," Trout said.

The sky turned the color of sheet tin, and off toward the arroyo they could already hear the coyotes and wolves cussing over the carcasses of the horses.

Jim felt a grim hatred for whoever had killed those animals, but he was pretty certain it wasn't old Hairy Legs. He imagined the old man sitting on the bank of the Pecos River eating his fish skewered over a hot little fire, washing it down with rotgut. A man like him had to feel like he was the last of his kind on the face of the earth, and Jim could relate to that.

Finally Trout reckoned he'd worn out his welcome, which he more or less had, because a little of Trout always went a long way. He stood and thanked Luz again for her hospitality and went and brought his horse up to the side of the porch in order to make an easier mount. Luz watched him with a certain wonderment, felt sorry for his horse, to have to carry all that weight around.

"I'll keep sniffing around for your horse killer," Trout said, his bulk settling down onto the saddle. "But I can't promise you whoever it was will ever get caught. Even human killers hardly ever get caught in these parts. Lincoln County is attracting the worst of the worst because those criminal heathens know there's not enough law to cover it all. Somebody like the Kid gets put down like the dog they are, and there are three more just like him, or worse, to take his place."

"I appreciate your riding out with me today," Jim said.

Trout belched and looked at Luz now sitting silent, her attention focused toward the arroyo. She was almost ghostly in her presence, he thought, but a beauty nonetheless. It was too bad about Hector; the fact that he'd left behind a fine young woman. Jim was one lucky son of a bitch, because Luz also owned her own place there in town. Trout imagined himself with a land-owning young widow like her. It would be a real sweet deal.

"You're a lucky son of a buck," Trout said. "Have you a woman like that."

"I know it."

Trout clucked the horse into a trot and rode off toward Domingo.

"I never cared much for that man," Luz said when they sat back down again, Jim watching the shrinking shape of the lawman as he went trotting up the road toward town.

"Trout's all right," he said. "If you can get past his mouth."

She put her hand on his knee and let it rest there. It was a comforting thing to have it there.

"You want to go inside?" she said.

"Not just yet."

"I hate that this has happened. That you lost all your horses."

"I'll find others."

"Still . . ."

"I know."

They sat there for a while longer in the cooling air now that the bank of clouds had partially blocked the heat of the sun. A gentle wind played along the porch. It was hard if not impossible to say what the night would bring, weather-wise or otherwise.

"I was thinking of asking you to marry me," he said. He said it so casually, she wasn't sure if she heard him correctly, or if it was just something she imagined him saying.

There was an awkward moment of silence. Then a meadowlark trilled and the silence was broken.

"Is this something you've been thinking about for a while, or just today," she said.

"A while. I was going to say something this morning, but then we sort of got wrapped up in other things."

She saw a smile playing at the corners of his mouth as he stared off like they were just this long coupled couple talking about how the garden or something was doing.

"There is something I've never asked you," she finally said.

"What is that?"

"If you've ever been married before."

"I never was," he said. "Never even came close. Seems I always fell in love with the wrong women when I fell at all—which I want you to know wasn't that often." Then he looked steady at her and added: "Till now."

"And you think I'm the right woman?"

"I could use another cigarette, and maybe a little bit more of this whiskey, only without so much water in it, couldn't you?"

She waited silently until he went in the house and
came out again carrying the half-empty bottle and
his makings.

"You want a refill?" he said.

"No, I've still got some."

He poured himself a little, then set it on the floor
of the porch while he fashioned himself a cigarette
and lit it.

"You don't have to give me an answer right
away," he said. "I just thought you should know
what I've been thinking about."

"Are you straight out asking me if I'd marry
you?"

"I guess that's what I'm asking, yes."

"I'd like to think about it a little."

"I figured you would. Just thought I'd mention it
so you could begin thinking on it case you needed
the time."

"Yes, well . . ."

He smoked his cigarette and she smoked hers
and they sipped the whiskey and listened to the
savagery way off toward the arroyo—the growls
and snarls as the predators had at the bodies of
the horses. *Something dies, something lives*, he
thought. *It's the way it is*. And they were grate-
ful for each other's presence when all the rest of
everything seemed to be ravaged by the teeth of the
hungry and wanting.

"Maybe we should go inside now," she said.

His heart felt heavy as she led him into the bedroom and undressed. The last of the day's light sliced through the window to caress her body, to shimmer in her black hair. He knew he had to let go of the one thing in order to enjoy the other.

But it wasn't until she touched him that he could.

Chapter Eight

When he went out in the morning the old breed, Hairy Legs, was there on the porch, sitting cross-legged, a ratty wool blanket pulled round his shoulders, the big ratty-looking straw sombrero perched on his head.

"The hell," Jim said, surprised to see him there.

"It was a long walk," Hairy Legs said in surprisingly good English, his voice rattling like gravel in a pail.

"No shit. You had to have walked all night to get here."

"Plenty of moon to see by. No problem."

"Didn't know you spoke the white man's tongue."

His slash of a mouth drew into a wry smile as much as he was capable of it.

"The white devil who wears the metal star likes to show off when we talk, uses half-assed sign language and Mexican with a little Apache thrown in, so I let him. You got something to eat for a poor old Indian? I'm hungry." He rubbed his belly.

"Sure."

"I could eat one of those chickens," he said, looking toward the coop.

"Chickens lay eggs and we tend to eat the eggs and save the chickens till there is a need."

"Makes sense. Eggs is okay."

"I'll see what my woman can fix up."

The breed stood with some little effort, keeping the blanket tight round his shoulders and said, "I'll come back when it's ready."

Jim watched him trudge off toward the ridge where his two friends, Tom and Antonia, were buried, then went in the house. Luz was just slipping into her cotton blouse.

"We have company for breakfast," he said.

"Don't tell me Trout has come back?"

"No, it's that old half-breed Apache Trout wanted me to hire to track whoever killed the horses."

He saw the puzzlement in her dark eyes.

"You attract some of the oddest people to your door," she said.

"You're telling me."

"You think you can trust him?"

"I don't know. Trout thinks maybe it was him who killed the horses. He carries a big enough knife, but I don't think it was him. He doesn't have the strength, and besides, it just doesn't seem like it's in his makeup—a thing like that."

Now she looked concerned as she tucked the ends of her blouse inside her long skirt.

"What if you're wrong?" she said. "What if he's come back this time to kill more than just horses?"

He shrugged.

"Don't you think if that was his intent he would have tried it in the night instead of sitting out there on the porch?"

"My father told me when I was a child that the Apaches eat horses," she said.

"I've heard that too. But I don't know if it's true."

"And now he's here to share our table?"

"Just don't offer him anything that looks like horse." It was a bad joke but one that broke some of the tension.

It caused Luz to roll her eyes.

"The Apaches killed one of my grandfathers," she said. "This was a long time ago, before there were very many whites around here. My grandmother used to tell me that when she and my grandfather were young there was lots of raiding going on both sides of the border between the Mexicans and the Apaches, stealing each other's horses and women and even children. I was always afraid the Apaches would come and steal me."

"I'm glad they didn't."

She still looked uncertain.

"I can ask him to leave," Jim said, "if it will make you feel more at ease."

"No. I think maybe my grandmother told me those things partly to scare me so I'd be a good child."

"Were you a good child?"

"Yes, until I ran away with Hector."

"I didn't know you ran away to get married?"

"You never asked."

"You must have loved him very much to elope like that."

"I did. I would have run away to the moon with him."

He saw a brief light of old memory in her gaze for the now dead husband, recalling, he was sure, those early times, perhaps even the very night they ran away together, and all the days after when love was still new and unscarred by argument and discord.

"I bet he was a good man, your husband."

"He was. And I still have love for him in my heart." She drew near Jim then and put her arms around him. "And I have love for you too and I don't ever confuse the two loves, just so you know."

"I know."

She kissed him, and he felt the ripple of desire begin all over in his blood. Like wobbling fire wire in a dry wind. It always amazed him a little, the effect she had on him, and he only hoped it was the same for her as well.

They went out into the other room, and she

started a fire in the stove and he went and gathered some eggs from the hens in the coop. The rooster strutted around and acted angry and he said, "You son of a bitch, you better keep doing your job or I'll feed you to that old Apache breed," and laughed at the thought.

He took the eggs in to Luz and went back out on the porch looking off toward the ridge, where he saw Hairy Legs up there by the gravestones walking around. He wondered if it *was* possible that the Apache was a horse killer, and if so, *why* he would have done such a thing. He didn't know much about Indians except the few ragged little bands of Comanche he'd helped run to ground in Texas when he was a still-wet-behind-the-ears young Texas Ranger working under Cap'n Rogers. But he remembered tales the Cap'n had told him and the other boys about what fierce fighters those Comanche were, how brave they were, and in Jim's few encounters with them, he learned the Cap'n was right about Comanche as he was about almost everything else. It was mostly just shoot and run with them. They would fire back and forth at each other and then the foe would disappear into the landscape or cross the Rio Grande into Mexico. Wasn't any of the young Rangers unhappy to see them not stand and fight to the death. They were hell of horsemen too, Jim knew that much, and even Cap'n Rogers gave them their due when it came to being horsemen.

"Those boys ride like they're half horse themselves." High compliments from a pretty fair horseman himself.

But Jim also had heard that Apache, unlike the Comanche, weren't that fond of horses. Now whether it was true they rode a horse till it dropped, then drank its blood and ate its flesh if they had the chance, he couldn't attest to, but he'd heard such stories from ex-cavalry soldiers who claimed to have fought them in southern Arizona—old men with walrus mustaches and big bellies who'd tell stories for the price of a glass of ice beer.

One old boy Jim met even claimed he was the sole survivor of Custer's command at the Little Big Horn and was writing a book on it. Course nobody in the place believed a damn word of it, but they all bought him a round anyway because he was, in the main, a sad specimen.

Jim saw Hairy Legs bend and look at the inscriptions on the headstones. Whether he could read English or not was in question. Then he saw the breed reach inside his blanket and come out with something and shake his hand as if scattering seed.

A bank of dark clouds that held the promise of more rain or snow approached from the north, kicking up a little chill wind. Hairy Legs ambled back to the house.

"You drink coffee?" Jim said.

The old man nodded.

"Put some sugar and whiskey in it and I'll drink it all day," he said.

Jim went inside and poured two cups. Luz said breakfast was about ready; she'd sliced some bacon to fry with the eggs and had set a pan of biscuits to bake that made a man want to sit down and just enjoy it all. Jim spooned in some sugar from the little china sugar bowl but forwent putting any whiskey in it. Then he carried both cups outside and handed the breed a cup. He took it in both hands and sipped with wrinkled lips after blowing off the steam.

"What was it you did up there?" Jim said, nodding toward the ridge.

"Made tobacco sacrifice to honor the dead."

"That was considerate of you."

He looked at Jim like he'd just stabbed him in his old heart with a rusty blade.

"You can hear spirits up there," Hairy Legs said. "Hear the dead speaking in the wind. They tell me there is a storm coming, plenty of snow. I read it on the moon last night too. How are those eggs doing?"

"About ready. You want to come inside to eat or out here?"

He shrugged.

"Too damn cold out here," he said.

They went in, and the old man looked at Luz like he'd known her all his life but hadn't seen her in a long time.

She wiped her hands nervously on her apron and took the biscuits from the stove and knocked them into a basket she then set on the table, filled plates with bacon and eggs and set them down on the table too.

Hairy Legs seated himself at one end of the table and began eating almost immediately. Luz and Jim set about their own breakfast while the breed ate with vigor and kept watching her.

He held up three fingers at one point. She held her breath for a moment.

"What is your meaning?" Jim said.

"Three is a good number," he said. "These are good eggs."

Luz's smile was one of near relief even if she was confused by the statement.

Then out of the blue she said, "Did you kill our horses?"

He looked at her with a steady, unflinching gaze, pulled his butcher knife from his waistband, and stabbed it into the surface of the table so hard, it was surprising he hadn't broken the blade. It wobbled a long time.

"No," he said, then reached for another biscuit. He ate every last biscuit except for one that he stuck inside his blue jacket pocket. Then he reached inside another pocket and took out three pebbles that were polished no doubt by a year or two of water running over them and set them on the table.

"For the food," he said.

"Good," Luz said, and took them and put them in her apron pocket, much to the old man's approval, judging by the pleased look on his face.

"You got tobacco?" he said.

"I thought you had some," Jim said, remembering what Hairy Legs said he had scattered on the ridge.

He shook his head.

"All gone."

Jim rose from the table and got his makings.

"We smoke outside."

Hairy Legs nodded and stood up.

"No ring," he said, looking at Luz.

"What?"

He pointed to Luz's finger.

"No husband."

"Husband's dead," she said.

He looked at Jim.

"This your new man?"

"It is."

"Too bad. I been on the scout for a wife. You cook pretty good and don't look too bad."

Luz tried hard not to show her discomfort.

"We'll go outside and smoke," Jim said again.

The wind had picked up considerable, and the bank of brooding clouds now bunched along the ridge like restless gray cattle getting ready to stampede. They completely blotted out the Capitans.

The two men rolled shucks. The Apache rolled his like he'd been doing it all his life, and Jim struck a match off the doorframe and held it cupped in his hands till Hairy Legs got the end of his smoke lit, then Jim lit his own before snapping out the match head.

"I might be able to help you find your horse killer," Hairy Legs said.

"How so?"

"Tracks."

"I already looked for sign, didn't find any, so did Trout when he was out here."

The breed let the smoke from his shuck curl around his face like one of the clouds coveting the ridgeline.

"I don't know about you, but that white devil with the tin star learned to track from the Crow. The Crow can't find their asses with both hands. You see what shit they got Custer into, don't you? I knew old Bloody Knife, Custer's Crow. Ha, ha, ha." He laughed, shaking his head. "You see what happened to Yellow Hair with them Crows leading him around."

"Why would you want to help me now when you didn't yesterday?"

"The spirits told me I should help you."

"What spirits?"

He pointed with his fat nose toward the ridge, where they could see the snow starting to fall.

"Those who sleep under the fancy rocks," he said.

"They said that, huh?"

"I don't know, maybe it was just the wind. Sometimes it's hard to tell. It could have been the horse spirits if it wasn't the ones sleeping under the rocks."

"If you want to help me I wouldn't turn you down."

"Ten dollars is my usual fee."

"The spirits give costly advice."

"Yes, no shit."

They smoked their shucks down. Jim pondered whether to head out in a coming snowstorm with a crazy old half-breed Mescalero Apache he'd have to pay ten dollars to, who didn't know if he heard voices of the dead, the wind, or slaughtered horses talking to him.

"How do I know you won't get me out there and kill me and come back and steal my woman?"

"I might. She's a pretty nice woman."

"Shit," Jim said, and rubbed out the stub of his smoke against the porch pillar. "How'd you get that one blue eye?"

"Maybe I'll tell you sometime."

"Shit," Jim said again and went into the house.

Chapter Nine

"Look yonder," Ardell said, pointing toward the rise of buildings.

"Town, all right."

"Can we get something to eat?"

"I guess you worked you up quite an appetite the other night."

Ardell didn't answer. He still had the voices of the horses in his head, crawling around in there like bugs, whispering to him, laughing at him, scratching at the inside of his skull.

"Roll your sleeves up. Somebody see you with all the blood, they'll think you murdered somebody."

The half-wit looked at his sleeves and rolled them up his fat arms till he couldn't roll them any higher. He then looked pleased with himself, like he'd accomplished a great thing.

"Don't be telling nobody about what you did

when we get there," Cicero said. "Don't be telling how you hear horses talking to you."

Ardell looked like he was about to start blubbering.

They rode on down the sloping road toward the town, the fetlocks of their horses crusted muddy, the slog and suck of their mounts' hooves a steady rhythm that sounded like fatigue.

They reined in at the Dollar Café. There were red-checked curtains in the windows and the smell of something cooking releasing itself from the stovepipe poked through the back part of the roof. Looked friendly enough and might have good eats.

They dismounted, Cicero making sure the gun riding his hip was covered by his frock coat, his dark trousers stuffed down into the tops of his muddy boots. Slapped his derby hat against his leg, knocking off whatever dirt it held, but most of the hat's stain was the whitish bands of sweat where brim met crown. He looked to the impartial observer like a drummer with a lump under his coat, unless they looked deep into his feral eyes. He wore a waistcoat of blue silk and had a derringer stuck down in one of the pockets as a backup for close-in work, something he admired whenever the opportunity presented itself. Killing a man at distance of say twenty paces was one thing; killing him in so close you could smell his cloying breath, look right into his fearful eyes was something else altogether. He almost preferred the close-in work for the intimacy of the thing. Like when he'd shot the doctor.

"Wipe off your boot soles," Cicero said to the half-wit before he opened the door. Ardell scraped them off on the edge of the boardwalk till Cicero nodded and then they went in.

There were just a few patrons. At that hour, the bulk of the morning crowd had already eaten and gone on its way. Cicero picked a table by the front window so he could watch the street. He liked keeping an eye on things, considered himself a class A observer of humankind. Had to be if you were in the killing business. A man's weakness shows itself in many ways—so does a woman's. He'd had women on his mind a lot lately. It had been three, four days since he'd lain with one—that whore in Fort Sumner—the little bow-legged one got passed around like a jug of cheap whiskey. Couldn't complain on the price, though, six bits and she'd do whatever you told her. Ugly little thing if you left the light on, so he didn't. Just snuffed the flame and told her to go at it and she did, and it felt about the same as if she'd been a pretty gal.

A waiter came over. A tall, thin man with whitish shaggy mustaches, a slight hump to his back. *What age will do to you,* Cicero thought. *Bend you like a mis-struck nail.*

"What'll it be, boys," the fellow said. Had a drawl to him sounded like he was originally from somewhere east of the Mississippi, which of course he was. What Cicero Pie couldn't have known about the waiter was, he had been a top hand in his younger days, had worked all the good ranches from here to the XIT in the Texas Panhandle. At one, he'd worked that spread as a stock detective tracking rustlers and shooting them like you would coyotes.

Rustlers and anything else that took the ranch owners' beeves. He was a crack shot with a Winchester rifle before his shooting eye went bad. Like looking through a glass of muddy water is how he described it. For a time, he had courted a woman named Maggie and come near to marrying her, but was so slow getting around to proposing, she married a storekeeper up in Tascosa instead, and it broke his heart so bad, he took to the bottle—crawled right down in it. Liquor led him to the life of drifting and more liquor until his days got all used up and he found himself down on his heels in the little New Mexican town working as waiter, dishwasher, swamper. He never thought it would come to this, but it had.

And now here he was, hard up against sixty, serving soup and steaks to fellows like these two, an oaf and a derby-wearing son of a bitch.

Cicero rubbed last night's sleep out of his eyes as he looked at the chalkboard with the menu written on it—half the words misspelled he did believe but could not be certain since he himself had never finished school beyond the fourth grade.

Bef for *beef,* *pootatoe* for *potato,* and so forth.

"I'll have a bowl of stew and a chunk of bread and some coffee."

The waiter looked at the half-wit.

Ardell shrugged.

"Me too, I reckon."

The waiter, who'd seen his share of blood in days quickly fading to mere memory, noted the blood on the rolled-up sleeves of the oaf. He wondered what sort of bloody mess the oaf had gotten himself into, but knew better than to linger, and turned and went toward the kitchen.

"That old fellow's got a humped back," Ardell said.

"Like he's got a big turtle under his shirt."

Ardell grinned at that.

Cicero's eye had come to rest on the thin, good-looking woman sitting across the way, sipping coffee and turning the pages of a Montgomery Ward catalog. She looked half Mex, half white, skin the color of honey. He stared till she looked up, which he knew she would. Their eyes met, and she held his gaze for a long moment, then turned back to her catalog as though she'd not seen him at all.

Little Paris thought as she looked over the latest women's fashions, *Now there is a pair of deuces if I ever saw any. More saddle bums, just what this old place needs. Why can't the wind blow me in a rich cattleman looking to get un-lonesome, looking to travel the world. No, all the wind ever blows in are types like them two—ferret-faced and big and dumb as mules.*

She reminded Cicero a little of that farmer's wife in Alamagordo that time. Just before he shot her. It wasn't exactly what anyone would call a case of mutual attraction, that's for sure. Took fifteen dollars off her and the old man combined, team of horses, nickel-plated pocket watch, some brooches, two shotguns, and a Russian model Smith & Wesson pistol. Sold the whole kit and caboodle in the very next town for eighty dollars hard cash.

The half-wit saw Cicero staring and turned his head.

"She's purty."

Cicero did not comment, wondering if his brother had ever had a piece of tail in his life and doubting he had.

"I've been thinking," Cicero said as they sipped their coffees the waiter carried to the table, saying as he did their food would be out shortly.

"What?"

"Maybe we ought to think about hanging round here for a while."

"I like it here."

"I don't mean in this café, I mean in this town."

The half-wit looked wounded.

"I know what you mean, I ain't an idjit."

"Since when?"

"What we gone do here?"

"I don't know yet, but did you see that big bank on the corner we passed?"

But the half-wit was staring out the window, his concentration the span of that of a child's. He was watching two boys playing tag out on the street. It made him want to go out and play with them.

"Anyway, I think we'll lay up here for a few days and see what's what."

Then the waiter brought their meals and set them down.

"Be anything else, boys?"

"Some of that," Cicero said, pointing with his chin toward the woman reading the catalog. "Why don't you just walk on over there and tell that little piece of tail to come join us."

The old man turned enough to recognize Little Paris, who came in regular this time of late morning; sometimes she came in even around noon for her breakfast. Generally she ate her breakfast alone. He always wondered if she ate alone on purpose or was it that her evenings and night life were taken up with all manner of men—he had even paid for a visit to her a few times—that she simply needed to not be around them in the light of day?

This old boy's rude comments filled his chest with hot anger. A man never openly insulted a woman in his day. Told himself were he younger, he'd offer to take the derby-wearing son of a bitch and that ox companion out back and whip a little respect into them. But the cot and one meal and two bits a day the job provided wasn't something to sneeze at, so all he said in reply to the man was, "Why don't you?" Then turned and walked away, still fevered with anger at the insult.

"You hear that mouth on him?" Cicero said. "Might be her old daddy, or something."

"She's purty," Ardell said again.

Cicero took two dollars out of his pocket and set it on the table, then said, "Come on, let's rent a room."

He made sure to pass near Little Paris's table but she did not look up even when he said, "We're staying over to the hotel if this town's got one. Come look me up and I'll show you something that will set your hair on fire." Grunted a laugh and walked out.

Even though she was a whore and she'd had worse than these two, they still smelled like horseshit and gunpowder, and she told herself she wouldn't screw either one of them for all the tea in China.

It set her to thinking about men in general and her life in particular. She had nearly four hundred dollars saved up. She figured at least two thousand for a fresh start if some wealthy rancher didn't come along first and offer to marry her—which none had so far in the three long years she'd been working out of the Cat's Paw. She still had her looks, but for how long? Next year, if she remembered rightly, she would turn thirty years old. The good news was there weren't any other decent whores in town to compare to her unless a man wanted himself one of those Chinese girls worked in Chinaman's alley. They all had bad teeth and diseased skin yellow as candle wax and didn't speak no English, so they couldn't even tell a fellow what a good fuck he was. She'd tried to get Trout to run them out of town, but the Chinaman paid Trout a percent to let him run them, and even Trout's love for her couldn't get him to budge on the matter.

"Man has to eat, Paris; besides, none of them hold a candle to you and you know it."

Yeah, she knew it, but still every dollar those Chink whores siphoned off was a dollar she could have added to her savings.

She knew Bilk would marry her, but he was too shy and content to stay right here in Domingo. Still, she would have considered it if he'd been older, a little closer to dying, a year or two, maybe, and she'd have waited him out. But Bilk was fairly young yet—he just acted old. And he was tightfisted except when it came to feeding Trout his meals for free in exchange for Trout reading dime romances to him.

Trout would probably marry her if she let it be known she was open to the idea. But Trout had no future and was himself looking for a woman who at the very least owned her own house. Trout was also by nature a lazy so-and-so, always insisting she get on top whenever he bought her services.

The one man she admired and held secret desire for was Jim Glass. But Jim had taken up with that Mexican Luz Otero, the widow. The rest of the men in Domingo were either too old, too poor, too ugly, or all three. Mostly all three. Take those two that just walked out. The one in the derby wasn't that bad-looking and about the right age, but he had the eyes of a devil, and she could feel trouble coming off him like heat off a woodstove, even if you put aside his nasty manner.

She told herself she had two choices: save up another thousand dollars or two, or fill her pockets full of rocks and walk into the river.

It was looking more and more that someday soon she'd have to go in search of rocks.

Chapter Ten

The breed stubbed out his cigarette and put the butt into a small drawstring leather pouch tied around his neck.

"Where'd you come by that army jacket?" Jim said, saddling his horse.

"Soldier gave it to me."

"Looks like it's shot full of holes."

He looked down at it, fingered one of the holes.

"He didn't need it no more."

"You kill him?"

"You got my ten dollars?"

Hairy Legs looked at the falling snowflakes; they were a wonderment to his skin each time he felt them, like the soft kisses of the kindest woman. His earliest boyhood memories were of snow, of seeing it in his grandfather's hair and watching it fall across a wide valley. His mother was a blue-eyed Spaniard captured in a raid across the border. His father wanted her because she had hair the color of corn silk and her blue eyes. Said she was sent to him first in a dream. She taught her son Spanish to go along with his Apache. Later he learned the English from whites, mostly the soldiers he scouted for. He liked the way they cussed. He liked the way they drank, too.

Jim went inside the house and told Luz there was a big storm coming but that he and the breed were going to go out and look for tracks anyway. He grabbed his mackinaw off the hook in the mudroom and shucked it on and took the gloves out of the pockets and pushed his hands into them.

"Why are you going with that crazy old fool?" she said. "I'm not sure I trust him."

He looked at her, then kissed her cheek.

"Damned if I know why I'm going with him either, but if there's a chance he can track down the ones responsible for what happened out there, then I've got to go with it."

"I wish you wouldn't," she said.

"What about the storm?"

Jim shrugged.

"Storm can't be helped. Longer I wait, less likely we are to cut some sign. Already have lost a day on this as it is. Best get going."

She took a deep breath and let it out.

"I should get home before the storm hits," she said.

"Little Jessie was one of the horses, remember?"

She looked suddenly sad. Hers was the little clay-bank sorrel, the last one he and Trout had dragged off to the arroyo.

"I'll bring you back a horse when I return," he said. "There's plenty of wood for the stove and some good books on the shelf if you get bored."

Reading had become a favorite pastime of his ever since he had bought the place and found a few old books left from when the Bowdres had lived there. He bought more over time as he could find them. Since meeting Luz, most of his free time had been taken up with her. A man only has so many hours in the day to get it all done.

"I'll mend your shirts," she said. "And whatever else needs mending." She still had not admitted to not being able to read.

"You did a good job on my heart," he said. "Mending it."

She smiled.

"Go on so you can get back here."

He stepped out into the swirling snow.

The Indian stood there with snowflakes collecting on the ratty brim of his straw sombrero.

"I only got one horse," he said to the Indian.

"I can count," he said.

"We can ride double."

"No, I'll walk."

"It'll make it a slow trip."

"What is the hurry? The horses are already dead, the one who killed them gone."

Hairy Legs looked at the stud.

"That looks like a good horse," he said.

"It's a real good horse."

"Wonder why that devil didn't kill him too?"

"This horse is too smart to let anyone just walk up and slit its throat. Hell, he still won't hardly let me even ride him, and I feed him."

Hairy Legs walked to the corral, keeping his eyes on the ground. He walked completely around, stooped at one point, and placed his hand against the newly fallen snow where there was the slightest pair of cups, then brushed away the flakes. Then he stood and pointed toward the ridge.

"He came in from that way," he said. "One man. White devil. Puts most of his weight on one leg. Right boot heel worn down. Got a bad left leg." Jim went over and looked and shook his head, because it didn't look like all that much sign to him.

He followed the breed as he walked toward the ridge, leading his horse by the reins. Hairy Legs moved steady for an old man, like it was something he'd done all his life and could do it better than anybody else.

As they crested the ridge the rake of the storm's wind hit them full on, the snow swirling so thick that when Jim looked back he could barely make out the house. Hairy Legs walked around examining the ground, then started down the other side angling off to his left. Jim followed him all the way to where the river bent back around in a wide arc and flowed southward again. He followed as the Apache turned and walked upstream for a hundred yards or so, where he stopped in a bosque of mesquite and cottonwoods that grew from the rich, water-fed soil. Again he squatted and examined the ground. Flakes fell in the river and got eaten up like mayflies by trout.

Hairy Legs brushed a patch of snow away with the palm of one hand over a snowy patch of ground and uncovered horse apples he crushed in his hand and put to his nose.

"He went that way. Kept his horse tied up here. You can see where the horse cropped off some of the mesquite here where he had it tied off. Shit here. Big horse."

Jim trusted the breed's judgment now.

"Okay," Hairy Legs said, extending his thick brown palm. "You pay me now. Ten dollars."

"We ain't found him yet."

"How hard is it be to find a man who limps and rides a big horse? Ain't you got no skills at all?"

"Could you at least tell me the color of the shirt he was wearing?"

"Blue," he said.

"How the hell you know that?"

Hairy Legs offered an off-grin.

"It's just a guess. Maybe his shirt is red or black."

"Great," Jim said. He reached into his pocket and took out the money and tried handing it over, but the breed waved it off.

"Silver," he said. "No paper."

"All I have is script."

"No good."

"Then you'll have to wait for me to go to the bank."

He shrugged.

"This storm is raising hell," Jim said.

Hairy Legs turned his face skyward, shrugged.

"I'll wait at the house while you get me my money."

"You make my woman nervous."

He grunted.

"I'll stay in that shed."

The storm was bearing down with a force now, the snow swirling so thickly they couldn't see more than a few feet.

"I'll have to talk to her about it."

"This one is going to be a bone rattler," Hairy Legs said, sniffing the air. "Could get ass-deep to a squaw."

They trudged back up the ridge and down again and walked back to the house. Hairy Legs waited outside. The wind was buffeting now; the snow already had laid down a fresh skin of white over the land, clots of it sticking to the rocks and grass.

Luz was sitting at the kitchen table sipping coffee. She looked surprised to see him.

"You didn't get very far," she said. "Did the storm get too much, or did that old man keel over and die?"

"No, he's outside. He found the tracks of the man who paid us a visit the other night. Only thing is, he wants silver instead of paper money. Means I'll have to go to the bank soon as this storm blows itself out, which don't look like anytime soon. He wants to stay around till I get him the money. How do you feel about that?"

The sound of the wind had grown to a low moan.

"Inside the house?"

"He can stay in the shed."

"It's already getting cold," she said, wrapping her arms around herself.

"I can give him some extra blankets."

"I feel terrible about it him staying out there. It would be treating him like a dog to have him stay in the shed."

"I can tell him he can come in and sit by the stove."

She looked uncertain. "Whatever you think is right," she said.

Jim stepped outside. Hairy Legs was squatting there against the lee wall, his eyes nearly closed.

"You can stay inside by the stove if you want, or I can give you extra blankets to stay out in the shed till this storm blows over and I can get you your money in town at the bank."

The breed opened his turtle eyes.

"Shed's fine," he said. "I wouldn't want your woman to be afraid."

"I'll get you the blankets."

The sky was nearly dark as night and it not yet noon.

Jim got the blankets and carried them outside and handed them to the Indian.

"Some whiskey would help keep the cold off."

"You get crazy when you drink?"

"Sometimes."

"Go on the warpath?"

"Used to. Too old now. Didn't ever scalp nobody. Got drunk once with Sitting Bull after he left that Wild West show he was in. Fucker could drink like he had two hollow legs."

Hairy Legs fingered one of the bullet holes in the jacket, let his fingers glide over the few remaining brass buttons as though he was recalling how he'd come by that jacket in the first place. There was something grimly interesting about his countenance.

"I heard about this society back East," he said. "They call it the Free Love Society. I think maybe I'll go see what it's all about. I've been thinking about it a long time. Maybe I'll go next week or the week after. It might take me a while to get there, but the spring is a good time to start if I'm going."

Jim didn't know how much to believe or not to believe.

"Tell your woman not to worry," Hairy Legs said. "I never did anything bad to people who didn't deserve it."

"That should make her feel swell."

Jim went back in and got the liquor bottle from the shelf and poured three fingers deep into a cup of coffee and took it back out and handed it to the breed. Snow was collecting against the edge of the porch, and they couldn't even see the ridge now or the tombstones or anything more than a few feet out from the house. It was a wet, heavy snow with flakes the size of poker chips. Jim went and unsaddled the stud and turned him out, made sure there was plenty of grain and water, then set the saddle inside the shed and looked around. There was enough room for a man to sleep comfortably among the saddles and sacks of grain. There were a few cracks the wind whistled through, but with extra blankets it shouldn't be too terrible. It was his choice, the way Jim figured. Some men, like some animals, weren't born to live inside.

He stepped out and crossed the yard to the lee side of the house again, where Hairy Legs squatted on his heels sipping his liquored coffee.

"You sure about staying in the shed?"

He nodded.

"Well, I'll leave the latch undone in case you change your mind and want to come in by the stove."

The Apache didn't say anything but trudged off

to the shed carrying his cup, and within a dozen feet of distance between them he became like a ghost in the heavily falling snow.

Jim went into the house and shook the snow off his coat in the mudroom, pulled off his wet boots, then went over to the stove and poured himself a cup of coffee and found Luz sitting in the main room, a shawl around her shoulders. She'd lit all the lamps. Her gaze rose to meet his. Wind rattled the windows with the storm.

"Looks like we're in for a time," she said.

"Looks like."

"Spring snow can be the worst kind—get some warm days, plant your garden, get your hopes high, then it's like winter again, everything dead, killed off if it gets too cold."

"That's what I like about this country," he said. "It's unpredictable."

She stood.

"You want to just wait it out?"

"Guess we don't have any choice."

"You want to read a book?"

He shrugged.

"What do you want to do?" he said.

She went to the bedroom. He followed her. It was just one of those days when you had to turn lemons into lemonade.

Chapter Eleven

His true and Christian name was Tug Bailey. Long in the tooth now, slow of movement, step and fetch; that's all he was to the German and his fat wife who ran the Dollar Café. Two bits a day and one free meal for his labor. You do dis, you do dat. They weren't mean-spirited folks, just Old World folks who demanded a lot. And what right had they to demand anything of him who was born and bred in Texas and not come over on any ship?

Well, he sat out back in the snow and smoked his shuck and thought about everything, his squandered life, death waiting just up the street one way or the other, how he'd let love slip through his fingers a time or two, living in one room of somebody else's place and no money in the bank. But what set the fire under his thinking and got it to boiling was the insult that derby-wearing son of a bitch had tossed Little Paris's way and how he didn't do a thing about it. His younger days he would beat the man down who insulted a woman—any woman.

Maybe Little Paris was a whore and maybe she wasn't a preacher's wife or even some cowboy's ma. But she was by God a woman, and where he came from, womanhood meant something no matter what the occupation. Whores were women just didn't have a piece of paper saying they were married to this one or that, the way he saw it. His own ma had raised him right, respectful of folks, womenfolks most especially.

So he sat there smoking and stewing what life had gotten to, the way things had changed since he was a kid, how the whole world seemed to have gone to hell, the roughnecks and ruffians, the profane and low dogs, and it just set the fire a little higher in him, got his blood boiling the way it hadn't boiled in years—all of it just spilling over and he couldn't say why this time and not some other, except it was what it was.

Then little one-eared Tommy Nettle came by, always skulking about in the alleys looking for some bit of food somebody might throw out in the trash, especially back there of the café, and he saw Tug Bailey, the café's waiter and dishwasher, sitting there smoking a shuck, wearing his old Stetson pulled down to the tops of his ears and his apron still tied on, and looking for all the world like a man lost inside himself. Like he too had been tossed out with the garbage.

"Whatcha doin'?"

"What's it look like?"

"Smoking."

"Well, that is by God what I'm doing."

Tommy Nettle, town sot, indeterminate age, but younger than him, Tug thought, and just as worse off. Still, Tommy had some spokes left in his wheel if he didn't drink himself to an early grave before they all got busted out. Run hard, die young, ain't that what they all said?

"Yes sir, I can see that's what you're doing, smoking. Yes sir."

"You want a shuck?"

"Yes sir, I surely do. Yes sir."

Tug handed the sot his makings, but the sot's hands shook so bad from the whiskey tremors, Tug took them back and fashioned the sot a cigarette before he spilled all the tobacco, then held a match flame steady to it till it caught.

"Thankee, thankee." The sot had a habit of repeating everything he said.

"You look sour as an old bull," the sot said. Tug looked at that side of the sot's head where it was missing an ear.

"How'd you lose that ear anyway?"

The sot grinned and shuffled his feet. His old coat was frayed so bad the elbows were clean out. No laces in his shoes, skin grimy as an unwashed fly-specked window.

He reached up where the ear was as though he

didn't even know it was missing, grinned a mouthful of shoepeg corn teeth.

"Man caught it off with a razor," the sot said.

"Why'd he do that for?"

"I was fighting with him."

"What were you fighting over?"

"Hell if I can remember. We was both drinking pretty hard."

"Just like that, he took a razor and cut off your ear? You kill him for doing it?"

The sot shook his head.

"No sir, didn't kill him. Yes sir, yes sir. Clean off he cut it. Tried sewing it back on but it didn't take. Turned black as a raisin and fell back off. Sure is a cold son of bitch out here, ain't it?"

"It ain't that cold."

"Seems like it is. Snow in the spring. Whatcha make of that?"

"I seen worse. Snow just makes it seem colder'n it is."

"Yes sir, yes sir. It surely does. Wish it would hurry up and get spring and stay that way, don't you?"

"I don't give a fuck if it does or it don't."

"What's got you so het up?"

"Sons a bitches," Tug said grimly.

"What sons a bitches?"

"Some was inside a little earlier."

"They give you a hard time of it?"

"Not me—but they insulted Little Paris."

"The whore?"

"You know another Little Paris lives around here besides the whore?"

"No sir, no sir, I surely do not. How'd they insult her?"

"They just said the wrong goddamn thing to me is all."

"I don't get it then."

"No, you sure as hell would not."

"You don't have a nickel for a beer you could let me have, do you?"

Tug reached inside his trouser pocket and took out the two bits he'd earned yesterday and hadn't yet spent because there wasn't nothing he could think to spend it on. He had about everything was necessary: a cot to sleep on, tobacco, an extra bottle of whiskey.

"Here," he said, and gave the money to the sot. "Get yourself something warm to eat in you. Beer, you'll just piss out."

"Yes sir, yes sir, I surely will do that."

"And if you drink it up and don't get nothing to eat, don't come asking me for no more money. I ain't a goddamn bank."

"No sir, no sir, I surely will not."

The sot shuffled his weight foot to foot like he was standing on a hot plate.

"Well go on."

"What you going to do?"

"I ain't decided yet."

The sot went on.

But truth was, Tug *had* decided what he was going to do. Went inside, removed his apron, and set it on a table right in front of the German's fat wife.

"I quit, goddamn it."

The German came out of the kitchen when he heard his wife's high-pitched voice.

"What you do?"

"I quit."

"You vant more money, is that it?"

"Hell, ain't enough money in all the banks in San Francisco can make me do this kindy work even one more day. Cash me out, Dutchy."

The German paid him for the nearly half day of work because he saw in Tug's eyes a certain threat he'd not seen before. And when Tug was walking out, the German said something unfriendly that could have been a curse, but he barely heard it because his mind was all over something else entirely. There was something liberating about taking that apron off and quitting the damn old German and his missus. He didn't allow himself to think about tomorrow or the day after it. *You just got today now to think about,* he told himself.

He went down the street to Pablo's stables where he slept in a shed out back. It was small, but big enough for a cot and his old wood trunk he kept his clothes and such in. Had a Colt Peacemaker under his clean and folded shirts. A box of shells for it. He hadn't fired the gun in twenty years but had always made sure to keep it oiled and from rust.

He put fresh loads in the chambers, tucked it down the waistband of his trousers held up by a wide leather belt fashioned from an old razor strap. He caught a glimpse of himself in the storefront windows of Main Street when he passed by.

You look like a man means business, he said to himself. *You look like you used to look like before they tied an apron around you and put a broom in your hand and you sold that fine racehorse you used to ride and that good rope and all the rest. You look like a rooting-tooting son of a bitch is what you look like.*

He walked to the hotel and asked was there two strangers staying there.

Woody the clerk saw the gun in Tug's waistband and said, "Jesus, Tug, you got business with them?"

"I want to know if they're checked in, is all."

Woody was from out East somewhere, had an accent sounded like nothing Tug never heard before, sounded like northern birch and snow and ice on a pond and soft little hills. Woody featured himself as a poet, albeit a failed one, and would take his lunch at the Dollar Café alone, always reading a book or writing in a journal. Had spectacles he wore made it hard to make out his eyes behind the glare off the lenses. Tug didn't consider Woody no sort of man to speak of, but didn't hold nothing personal against him for his ways.

"I hope you're not planning on making trouble," Woody said.

"I come for an apology, is all."

Woody suddenly looked nervous, like a bank clerk with masked men coming through the front door.

"You're bound to get yourself killed, Tug, if you fool with those fellows."

"Maybe so, just tell me what room those sons a bitches are staying in."

"Tug . . ."

"Don't Tug me you little son a bitch."

"Now Tug . . ."

"Goddamn it, Woody, don't make me bust you in the mouth."

"No . . ." Woody held up both hands as though to fend off a blow that hadn't yet been delivered.

"What room?"

"Two-oh-one, top of stairs."

"Go and get the constable."

"Why, Tug?"

"Because I might have to kill those sons a bitches or they might have to kill me and I want an eyewitness to it whichever way it goes down."

"Yes sir!"

Tug unloosed his Colt and started up the stairs. Woody ran out the front door and down the street to the Cat's Paw, where he found Trout reading from the same dime romance novel he'd been reading from before Jim came and got him to go look for the horse killer.

"You better come on," he pleaded.

Bilk looked up the same time Trout did, both men having been engrossed in the lurid tale.

"Come on for what?" Trout asked.

"Tug's about to kill some men over to the hotel."

"What for is he intending on killing them?"

"Hell if I know, but you better come on quick."

"Jesus fuck Almighty!"

Trout unhinged himself from the bar stool. Trouble seemed to come and go like the weather—unpredictable as Nancy's goat. Could be nice one day and terrible the next or both in the same hour.

He went at as quick a pace as a man his bulk could go, trailing behind Woody, who was all arms and legs.

Tug rapped on the door hard with his fist.

"Who is it?" a voice called from the other side. "What you want?"

"I come to get an apology out of you!"

"What?"

Tug repeated his demand.

The door opened.

Cicero Pie stood there in his stocking feet and union suit. The big man lay stretched out on the bed like a felled ox.

"Now just what the fuck is it you're doing at my door?" Cicero said.

"You insulted that lady through me at the café and I want you to apologize."

"What lady? That Mex whore?"

"You apologize or get heeled."

The Mortician looked at the half-wit. The half-wit sat up, staring.

"You believe this?" the Mortician said.

The half-wit shook his head.

"What's he meaning, Cicero?"

The Mortician looked at the waiter.

"You got yourself a goddamn death wish, old man?"

"I guess I sure as fuck must."

"I guess you sure as fuck must, too."

"I'll be out in the street."

"I'll be right down."

"All right then."

"All right."

Tug turned and walked down the stairs, satisfied whatever it was about to take place would take place soon and all of life would change forever. He felt good, a warmness in his chest, a fire in his blood raging up again. He was by God if anything a man once more and not some goddamn waiter.

He went out and stood in the middle of the street, the snow falling all around him like a miracle.

Miracle of days, he thought. *Somebody is going to meet Jesus.*

Chapter Twelve

They made love, then slept, then woke again late in the afternoon of that day, and when he got out of bed and went to the window he saw it had stopped snowing and the sky was a mixture of blue with white smoky clouds. Sun sparkled in the snow so bright and clean it hurt his eyes to look at it. He could hear water dripping from the eaves into the rain barrel. Such was the vagaries of a spring day in New Mexico Territory.

"It's quit snowing," he said.

Luz rolled onto her side and looked at him.

"Yes," she said.

"Yes what?"

"Yes, I think I would like to marry you."

He turned from the window and smiled.

"I was hoping that you'd come to that decision."

"I thought about it but I knew the moment you

asked me that I would say yes. In a way, it feels as though we're already married."

"Guess that means I need to ride into town and buy you a ring."

"No, your word is good enough. Besides, I already have a ring at home that Hector gave me."

"No, I want to buy you one that's from me. No disrespect," he said. "But I want it to be a real wedding. We'll invite everybody we know and everybody we don't know. Have a real shivaree."

"It's not necessary."

He came to the bed and lay down beside her.

"That's the way I'd like it, Luz—a real honest-to-God wedding, let everybody know how I feel about you."

She smiled.

"It is the happiest of times and the saddest of times," she said, thinking about the horses.

"Whatever it is, we can get through it," he said.

"Yes."

He stood again and dressed and she watched him, then sat up herself and he watched her—her caramel brown body a study in womanly beauty, a body he so craved even when he thought he'd had all of it a man could possibly stand. He knew he could never get enough of her if he lived another fifty years.

"I love you," he said as she pulled a peasant's blouse over her head.

"I love you too, Jim."

It was the best kind of love, he thought, a steady, deep-down love he knew would always be there in him—a love like a river, one that always flows.

"I'll make us something to eat," she said.

"I'll go see how the breed is making out."

Hairy Legs had lain in the shadowy interior of the shed with its smell of saddle leather and harness and stacked bales of hay and bags of grain. He'd drunk his whiskey-laced coffee and felt its thin rivers of fire course through his blood. Cold all the time now that he'd gotten old. Wondered sometimes if he might freeze to death just from being cold all the time in his blood.

The wind had howled like some old wolf for a time, then eased to a whimper before falling silent altogether. Snow blew through the cracks of the boards at first, but he was nice and comfortably warm within the extra blankets. Only thing that would have made it cozier would have been a woman in there with him too. He couldn't even remember unless he thought on it hard how long it had been since he'd felt the warm flesh of a woman.

After the wind quit telling him things, he heard the yip and snarl again coming up from where the white devils had dragged the horses. He'd come right past the arroyo the night of his walk from his place to here. Had seen them down in there, ghostly under the moon, the shadowy dark bodies of the skulking canines and skirted wide, case they took it in their feeble brains to get something live on the hoof. Figured by now they'd have those horses et down to the shoes.

He remembered eating horse once. It wasn't very good. Not as good as buffalo or antelope. Not even as good as rabbit.

It was Three Fingers's old gray horse. Had died on him without known cause.

Three Fingers cut it up into big pieces and shared it with everyone. The piece he had eaten had been roasted over a fire. Tough to chew, real stringy. Wouldn't have et it at all except it was Three Fingers's sister gave it to him. Him and her drunk as dogs on a jug of liquor she'd stolen off a liquor drummer passed through and was diddling Hump Dog's widow at the time, his attention on his liquor stock being duly distracted by Hump Dog's widow's cries—an old trick she used. The drummer, a little round man with bugged eyes, squealed like a pig in his thrusting. Hump Dog's widow and Three Fingers's sister worked in concert whenever they could to steal whatever wasn't nailed down. Three Fingers's sister was named Sweet Grass. But there wasn't anything sweet about her except she usually had something to drink and the price wasn't overly steep for a man hard up for both liquor and a woman if he wasn't too choosy about either.

No, he didn't think he'd want to eat no more horse 'less he was starved.

The door rattled open.

"It's quit snowing," Jim said.

An almost angry light sliced in through the open door, sharp as a knife blade.

"You hungry?"

Hairy Legs thought about them horses being eaten by the coyotes and wolves and probably ravens too. Thought about Three Fingers's old gray horse that time, the taste of it not even able to wash away with Sweet Grass's stole liquor.

"Not so much," he said to the question of his hunger.

"My woman's fixing some grub."

Hairy Legs stepped out into the white landscape, looked around, his nostrils flaring with the scent of clean crisp air, the wood smoke coming drifting down from the chimney, carrying with it the scent of warm bread.

Off to the east he saw the hump of the storm, gray and moving swiftly, leaving in its wake a glassy blue sky with puffs of clouds like smoke from a pipe. The Capitans were once more visible.

"We'll eat something, then I'll go to town and get your money."

"What about the horse killer?"

"I'll never find him," Jim said. "This is big country. Men become like ghosts. Besides, with this new snow, it'd take a good piece of luck to pick up his trail again."

They ate a meal of cooked beef, onions, beans, tortillas, coffee.

"Good," Hairy Legs said when he finished, having forced away the thoughts of horse. He had an odor about him of smoke and grease and sweat and maybe blood, Luz thought. How much of other men's blood had the old Indian shed in his lifetime, she wondered.

He watched her closely; she didn't care for it but did not cut her gaze either; she did not want to show him any sign she was afraid of him or otherwise intimidated.

He liked her. He liked the man too.

"You come back with a horse, I'll go with you to find the horse killer," he said.

"What got you to change your mind?"

Hairy Legs looked at Luz again.

Jim noticed the look.

"Maybe I do it for her," he said.

"I can trust you not to do anything all of us will end up regretting while I'm gone?"

"Don't worry, I'll watch out for her."

"Thank you," Luz said, irritated. "But I don't need anyone looking after me."

The breed smiled in that way he had—an old, wrinkled walnut shell of a smile that was an unspoken history of all the women he'd known.

"Then I'll just sit outside and wait."

They stood from the table, and the two men walked outside and Jim saddled his horse, while Hairy Legs watched with those baleful, half-lidded turtle eyes as though his whole being was possessed of a great quietude. Hairy Legs sat on one of the porch chairs, the sun splashing down now turning the flooring warm enough, he could smell the wood planks.

The saddle leather creaked with Jim's weight.

"I'll be back in an hour."

The sun indicated the time was about three hours past noon. Jim started to rein his horse round, then paused and looked from Luz to the breed once more.

"Just so you know, I'm not a merciful man when it comes to a violation of me or my own," he said.

"Me either."

"Good, then we understand each other."

Jim turned the stud toward town. Something told him if he was to be violated again it wouldn't be the breed who would be the culprit.

And besides, Luz had the ten-gauge right there inside the front door, and he trusted she would use it if it came to that.

Amen for a strong woman.

Chapter Thirteen

The half-wit watched his brother strap on his pistol, check the loads, put a shell in the chamber under the hammer, the chamber he generally left empty so as not to shoot himself accidentally. He checked the belly gun he carried too in the pocket of his waistcoat. Going into a known gunfight, Cicero Pie liked to have all the lead available he could sling.

"I'm going to kill that goddamn old fool," he said to nobody in particular, the half-wit tugging on his big black boots.

"What about the law?"

"Fuck the law."

"We still going to rob the bank?"

"Sure we are. Fact is I'm thinking of sending for Hatch and them to help us rob it. Was thinking about it just now when that goddamn fool hammered on my door."

"Hatch and them?"

"That's right, you remember old Hatch and his cousin Willis, don't you?"

The half-wit nodded.

He remembered about old Hatch and Willis as come-and-go-as-you-please men who often appeared at their mother's place either together or alone. Fact is, last time Ardell saw either of them was when old Hatch showed up by himself, saying he was supposed to meet Willis in a couple of days. Only while he was hanging around, Ardell saw Hatch through the window of his maw's room standing there with his back to the window and his maw down on her knees in front of him. Old Hatch quivering like a fevered man, moaning like somebody had shot him through the backbone.

Ardell never said nothing to Cicero about it because his maw happened to stand up sudden and see him looking through the window. She approached him later that day—Cicero gone into town for dry goods and to get his drunk on—and warned him.

"What you saw earlier ain't what you think you saw," she said to him. Old Hatch was up in the spare room sleeping in the lazy heat of the day in spite of the greenhead houseflies that would worry a man out of his innermost dreams. "I know it looked funny, but the man provides us with a little money, and sometimes a body has to do what a body has to do to survive."

"What was you doing with him, Maw?"

"Measuring him for a new pair of trousers, son.

That's how I make a little money off him—making him new trousers." Then she waited a moment before adding: "Sometimes you think you see something that seems like something else, but that's what I was doing, measuring Hatch for some new trousers, and that's all I was doing."

The half-wit tried to remember if he ever saw Hatch wearing a new pair of trousers. He couldn't think of a time when he had.

"Anyways, I don't want you to say nothing to your brother," she said. "You know what a hothead he is, how he's always so quick to jump the gun. If he thought I was doing anything untoward . . . well, just don't say nothing."

Ardell stood mute.

"You hear me, son. You don't say nothing to Cicero."

"Yes, Maw."

"Now let me go fix you something good to eat and here's a dollar."

"What you giving me a dollar for, Maw?"

"'Cause you're a real good boy and 'cause you won't say nothing to your brother about me measuring old Hatch for some new trousers, will you now?"

"No Maw."

She patted him softly on the cheek then and fixed him a nice meal of fried chicken, which he and old Hatch ate across the table from each other, old Hatch looking for all the world like what he was: a shiftless soul given to getting by without ever having to hold a regular job anybody ever knew of. Yet him and Willis, every time you seen them, was flashing around money and drinking like they'd bought the last whiskey keg ever made. Willis always had pocket money.

Cicero had told Ardell, when Hatch had shown up at the family homestead for the first time since their daddy had run off, that Hatch had been in prison for robbing a string of whorehouses in Oklahoma. Him and Willis. Cicero saying how the law never did catch up with Willis.

"Willis is just as bad as old Hatch when it comes to criminal activity. And I bet they stole more than money from them cathouses, too," Cicero said with a wicked little grin. Last the half-wit heard, old Hatch and Willis were living in El Paso, Texas, and running a gambling joint down there together.

"I don't like him none too much," the half-wit said when Cicero mentioned he was thinking of wiring him.

"Hell, old Hatch's all right. I think him and Willis would jump at the chance to rob a good bank like this one here. I'm thinking we pull this one off, we'll just go into the bank-robbing business altogether, like old Jesse and Frank done."

"Ain't Jesse dead and Frank in jail?"

"Goddamn right, which means there's room for a couple of enterprising men like us. You and me will be the new Frank and Jesse, and old Hatch and

Willis will be like the Youngers."

Ardell felt glum; the image of his maw on her knees in front of old Hatch still felt burned in his mind like a woodcut.

"Anyway, I got this business needs taking care of," Cicero said. "Got this reputation to uphold— you know, *the Mortician*." Grinned and walked out of the room with a pistol riding high up on his hip, confident he could pull and fire it before the old fool ever knew what hit him.

Tug Bailey waited in the street for the sons a bitches to put in an appearance. He faced the front door of the hotel, the snow having now stopped and the first sun breaking through the suddenly parting clouds.

People who had been on the streets stopped and stared at the old waiter standing out there intent as a bird dog on point, a big pistol in his belt.

"Looks like there might be a fight," somebody said to somebody else.

"Looks like."

Then they saw Trout rumbling up the street, the bulk of him not running, but walking at a quicker than his usual pace. Trout had sent Woody off to go find his deputies when he heard Tug was fixing for a fight with two strangers recently arrived in town.

"Who are they?" he'd asked Woody as they exited the Cat's Paw, "these two men Tug wants to shoot?"

"You aren't going to believe how they signed their names—least the one did," Woody said.

"I ain't got no time for guessing games, poet."

"Signed their names, 'The Mortician and his Assistant.'"

It stopped Trout up short. *The Mortician?* He'd heard that name bandied about. A first-rate man killer if everything he'd heard about him was true, and he had no reason to believe it was not. Of course the West was full of self-appointed bad actors, men calling themselves Kid this and Kid that, Wild Bill this or Wild Bill that. Stuff you'd read in dime novels. But some of these fellows actually *were* bad.

"You sure that's how they signed?"

Woody nodded, and that's when Trout told him to go round up his two part-time deputies and get them down to the hotel quick.

Trout came around the corner and saw Tug standing out in the street, bent and old but standing steady as a statue, facing the front doors of the hotel.

He called to him from a distance of forty paces or so, not wanting to come up behind him sudden like and get his ownself shot by a touchy old fool with a gun.

"Tug, I want you to walk away from here," Trout shouted.

"Go find you another hand to deal, Constable, this one's already dealt."

"Now, Tug, you're just going to go and get yourself shot all to pieces—two of them against one of you. Who'll serve me my coffee tomorrow morning if that happens?"

Tug threw the constable a sidelong look.

"I guess you'll just have to get off your fat ass and get your own coffee, Trout. I'm all finished with that nonsense."

Trout never knew the quiet Westerner to be anything other than quiet and unassuming like all the other old cusses he'd ever met; men with quiet histories, almost to the point of not even being noticed. This was a whole other side of him Trout was seeing.

"Tug, why you want to fight these fellows?"

"They insulted Little Paris is why."

"Well now, how'd they do that, Tug, insult her?"

"Said something ungenteel about her. I stood by and didn't do nothing then, but I'm going to do something about it now."

"She's a whore, Tug. I doubt if she'd even noticed or cared."

"I ain't come here to carry on a conversation with you, Trout. Why don't you just walk on down the street and get a haircut and come back later."

"Tug . . ."

Then two men came out through the front doors of the hotel: one big as a house and the other smallish, but wearing the flap of his frock coat thrown back and tucked behind the butt of his revolvers—

smallish, but those big pistols made him every man's equal.

"I'm here, you old goddamn idiot," Cicero said, stepping down from the walk into the muddy street, little patches of as yet unmelted snow still lying about.

The air was cool on the skin, like fresh spring water.

"I'll give you one more chance to apologize," Tug said, already knowing he was going to be shot, that such men never apologized for their bad behavior. His stomach knotted, seeing the man armed now and that big oaf with him probably also armed under his coat. Tug figured maybe the bullet's punch would be quick and lethal and he'd never even feel it. Anyway, he told himself, he'd closed all the doors he'd walked out of since he quit his job at the café, and that was okay with him. Now he had just one more door he knew he must step through—the one that led to a great room of eternal darkness. And maybe if he got lucky, he'd take this derby-wearing son of a bitch with him. The thought caused his right hand to tremble a little more than what he liked. No sir, it sure wasn't the old days, now was it. He caught a glimpse of one-ear Tommy Nettle there at the mouth of an alleyway ran along between the hotel and the jeweler's, nipping from a pint bottle of something, and it pissed Tug off the damn fool had spent the money he gave him on booze instead of something warm in his belly.

"And I'll give you one chance to get on your knees and beg me not to shoot you, you old bastard," the Mortician said.

"Shit," muttered Trout.

"Hold up, boys," he called, standing there in front of Dr. Salvador's dentist office.

The armed stranger jerked his eyes toward the lawman.

"Stay the fuck out of this, dad."

"I'm the law and if you don't disarm yourself—"

"You'll what?" the Mortician said, cutting off Trout's threat. He wasn't in any mood for threats. That wasn't how he operated. It wasn't how he *ever* operated.

Trout's own gun seemed a hundred miles away. But now he was caught up in things and couldn't just walk away. That was the thing about taking other folks' money to defend them; you couldn't always just walk away and make believe their troubles weren't your own.

Trout's musing lasted less than a second, for he knew men like the one standing across the street from him did not hesitate. And yet he knew too he was too far away to hit any goddamn thing with a pistol. He needed to close the space by half. And yet that silly old man stood between him and the Mortician.

"Somebody's going to end up dead here!" Trout warned, stepping down off the walk into the same street Tug Bailey stood in, for there wasn't any other way of doing it. If he couldn't hit the Mortician at this distance with a pistol, it was unlikely the Mortician could hit him either. Closing the gap between them was the only way to do it.

"No shit!" the Mortician said. "But it ain't going to be me."

He pulled his revolvers so slick and fast, neither Tug nor Trout could react fast enough. Tug got his own gun only halfway out of the waistband of his pants, but that was all she wrote. Three bullets punched into his body so hard it knocked him backward five or six steps, just walked him backward like he was dancing with an invisible partner. Tug's finger jerked the trigger on his double action, firing a round directly into the mud near his foot, then his hand and fingers didn't seem to want to work anymore and he sat straight down on his ass. *Whump!* His breathing coming hard. Like somebody had set a load of bricks on his chest. He could feel the mud soaking up through his crotch, cold and wet. Or was it blood?

Oh, it hurt a hell of a lot worse than he thought it would. Way worse.

Trout saw it coming even as he made an effort to cross the street and close the gap. It was like he was in some sort of play, like the one he'd seen in Chicago that time when Billy Cody and Texas Jack and Ned Buntline performed. Where they shot it out with the Indians—Billy giving a long-winded speech first, forgetting his lines.

Trout had his own gun out now, holding it straight

out from him, his arm extended, his thumb drawing back the hammer of the single action. He pulled
the trigger, but sure as shit missed the smallish man
partly enveloped in a cloud of his own making. This
he knew when the Mortician swung round his way,
not more than three, four inches difference in his
stance from when he shot Tug. Just enough. And
something that felt about like a railroad spike drove
in with a nine-pound hammer slammed into his
shoulder.

But he was het up now, and he thumbed the hammer back and fired again and again, thinking he
had to knock the son of a bitch over with one of
those shots. But he never did, and in the end the
Mortician was still standing and Trout was tasting
mud. He didn't even know what happened, really. It
was just sudden. He was standing there, firing away,
and then he was facedown in the street. Couldn't
feel his legs.

Some woman was screaming. It could have been
Little Paris. Or it could have been somebody else.
Sounded just like some respectable woman who'd
seen something she ought not have and cut loose
her horror, which is exactly what it was. Woody
also saw it all, committed it to memory, knowing
someday he'd write a poem about it, or perhaps an
article for *Harper's Weekly*. Already had some of it
written down in his mind:

This day, with the weather so odd and strange as

to be something to behold—one minute snowing as if a blizzard, and the next, the sky bright and clean, the sun warm upon the inhabitants, death was dealt in the streets of Domingo . . .

"You killed 'em, Cicero, you killed 'em both," the half-wit said.

"No, they ain't dead yet, neither one. Look at how they're still wiggling about like worms somebody spilled out of a tobacco can."

Tug sat there gripping handfuls of mud, clawing at the earth like he was trying to get inside of it—a desire that he sensed would soon be fulfilled. But it was awful, the waiting part, the pain that excoriated with every passing and struggling breath. Wasn't no way to get around the pain, and what was even worse than the pain itself—knowing he couldn't do nothing to escape it, that it would ride him right on out of this world.

He saw out of the corner of his eye the constable lying facedown and couldn't quite figure it out.

"Trout," he muttered. "Trout . . ."

Trout himself muttering: "Sweet Jesus, I've been slain. Sweet Jesus . . ."

Cicero Pie eyed the onlookers to see if there were any more challengers to him. And there would have been had not the two deputies Woody tried to summon stayed in their houses, refusing to come. Wives saying, "It's too much to ask of you to go out there and get yourself murdered for fifteen dollars a month and no regular work. It's too much." The two men glad their wise wives had talked them out of it.

And when nobody made their play, Cicero Pie, the one called the Mortician, reloaded his pistols, dropping the empties there on the walk so that they clattered like spilled coins, then calmly stepped into the street and walked over to Tug Bailey and shot a round through the top of his skull. Then took three more steps to the fallen constable, his shadow falling long over Trout's bulk, and stood for a moment blocking out the sun.

"Just so you know"—and he addressed the onlookers as well as Trout—"I ain't one to let my enemies suffer unmercifully . . ." Then shot him too, in the back of the head.

Woody looked round to see if the other two deputies were on their way, but saw nary a soul coming up the street, and his heart sank along with those of all the others.

"That's it then," the Mortician said and holstered his revolvers, and turned and said to the half-wit, "You see that?"

The half-wit nodded.

"All right, then."

They walked over to the telegraph office like two men going for a stroll on a pretty day.

Chapter Fourteen

He rode with a single thought: horses. Domingo lay ahead. Hopefully the Mexican would have extra horses he could buy. There were wild horses to be had, but it would take time to locate and capture them. They'd be farther south still, grazing on the grasses before moving north onto the benchlands as the weather grew warmer. Until he had time to go after them, he'd have to buy a couple—one for Luz and one for the breed to ride.

He rode at a steady lope, the weather clearing, the sun warm on his face and the backs of his hands. He rode with a purpose, the horse's hooves kicking up muddy clots.

Once he reached Domingo, he rode straight to the stables run by the Mexican, Pablo, who also dug graves at the cemetery with the Negro, Black Bob. Jim reined in, dismounted, and tied off. Nobody was around. He looked over the stock in the corral and back in the stalls, some poor-looking horseflesh at best; mostly horses the Mexican rented, hard-mouthed, some broke to rein with barbed wire. They whickered and swished their tails because of the greenhead flies that were already abundant this early in the year. A couple of horses finally took his eye: a gray filly for Luz, and a broad-chested dun should work for the breed—the best two in the lot. He figured not more than fifty dollars for the pair. Stood waiting patiently for the Mexican to put in an appearance, and when after ten minutes he still hadn't, Jim remounted and rode into the heart of town to look for him.

He got as far as the hotel when he saw what at first seemed like a large puddle of red rain, then quickly realized it was blood. There were few pedestrians. He rode up one block to the Cat's Paw and dismounted and tied off and went in. You wanted to learn anything, you talked to the bartender.

Bilk was behind the bar serving several galoots standing facing him. They were all talking loudly.

Jim worked his way to the bar and said, "Pardon me, but I'm looking for the stable owner, Pablo. Anybody seen him?" Funny, but Trout wasn't at his usual station end of the bar.

"He's helping to dig graves," Bilk said. "Trout and that crazy old coot Tug Bailey got themselves shot to death less than an hour ago."

It was a shocking piece of news.

"How'd that come about?"

"Tug took offense at something a stranger in town said about Little Paris and challenged them to a gunfight." Bilk shook his head. "I guess he wasn't no good at math."

"How's do you mean?"

"Should have known two is a greater sum than one."

"That's what it was, he went up against two men?"

"Just about, except Trout got kindy in the middle of it. That fellow shot them both dead."

"Which fellow?"

"One over the hotel. Him and some oaf he's got with him, only the oaf didn't so much as draw a gun. All the shooting was performed by the one— little fellow with snake eyes."

"That so?"

Bilk nodded.

"'Tis a damn fact."

"Trout wasn't too bad with a gun."

"Not good enough it seems."

"Fair fight? Anybody here see if it was a fair fight?"

Men nodded as they sipped their beers and shots of whiskey.

"'Bout as fair as you'd expect, except it wasn't," one of them said.

"I don't follow your meaning?"

"You could just tell that feller was a killer of the first rank. Tug never would have stood a chance even with a lesser man, old as Tug was. Trout, well, Trout's mettle was tougher than his aim. This feller was about half his age and cool as a block of ice when it came to pulling the trigger. Trout got off three, four shots but missed ever' one. That fellow hit him both shots he fired and put him down."

"I'm sorry to hear the news," Jim said. He started to turn and walk out, to find Pablo over at the cemetery and bargaining for two horses. It was a troubling situation about Trout. Tug Bailey he knew only slightly, never said more than hello to the man, figured he was like a lot of old boots who'd once been too proud to do any sort of work couldn't be done from horseback, but eventually found themselves taking what they could get. Maybe it beat an old-folks home—going down fighting for what you thought was right.

Then Bilk said, "They was murdered is what they was. I don't think he intended to kill them outright . . ."

Jim turned to face the barkeep.

"Say it plain."

"That fellow shot them bad enough to put them down but not kill them right off. I think he wanted them to know it was coming. He put them down and then walked over and gave them each a kill shot, like you would a mule deer or something you were hunting."

The others nodded and looked into their glasses.

"They might have lived if he hadn't delivered the coup de grâce. Hard to say but they might have . . ."

"Nobody tried to stop it?"

Every man in the place seemed to shrink a little from the question. Silence all up and down the line until Bilk said, "Who you think was going to stop it—a thing like that, except somebody didn't care about drawing another breath his ownself?"

"He's right," a feminine voice from the shadows said. "Somebody should have stopped it."

They turned then, all of them, and looked at Little Paris sitting alone at a table.

"Didn't see you jumping into the mix," one of them said. Bilk felt ashamed she was even there, challenging them, challenging him directly, it seemed to him. Same as calling him out as a coward.

She locked her gaze with Jim's.

"Nobody did a goddamn thing," she said, "but watch that little son of a bitch murder Trout and Tug."

"Where they at now?" Jim said. "These fellows?"

She shrugged.

"What difference does it make? They're out there walking around free and upright, and Tug and Trout are laid out on blocks of ice. Nobody's going to do anything . . ."

He turned to the others. Nobody offered an answer. Nobody wanted to know where they were at now. Everybody content to drink their drinks and talk about it and stay inside for now. It was too late to find a man among them to do anything *but* talk about it; something they would do for weeks, or until the next thing worth talking about came on the scene.

"What happened with those deputies Trout employed?" Jim said. "How come they weren't backing his play?"

Finally a voice nearly as feminine as Little Paris's, but softer, spoke from the end of the bar. Jim recognized him as the hotel clerk, Woody something or other. What little light invaded the interior of the place reflected dully off his spectacles and their wire rims.

"They are registered at the hotel as the Mortician and Assistant," he said. "Trout sent me to get his deputies, but they never came . . ."

"Why didn't they?"

The young man shrugged.

"I don't know," he said.

"What's the matter with you people?" Jim said, his voice edged with anger and indignation. "You all just stand by and watch somebody murder your constable?"

Men shifted their weight, coughed, sipped their beer, said nothing in response. Jim felt disgusted with the lot of them.

"Have a good day, gents," he said sarcastically

and walked out. He rode up the street and past the hotel where Woody said they were staying. What was it Woody said they registered as? *The Mortician and Assistant?* Seemed to him he'd heard something about such a man, maybe read about a fellow went around calling himself that, the Mortician. He had only a vague memory of it. But whoever or whatever they were, it wasn't up to him to mete out justice—to take up for a town of men who wouldn't take up for themselves. To hell with them all, he thought, and rode on to the cemetery, where he found the Mexican and the Negro, Black Bob, digging two graves side by side in sweaty silence except for the chunk of the pick, the chick of the spade.

"I need to buy a couple of horses if you're willing to sell," he said to the Mexican.

"Sí."

"Now, if you can break off your work here for a minute, I'm in a hurry."

"Sí."

Black Bob eyed the two of them warily. He got two dollars for each grave he dug. But nobody needed a grave here lately, and he was down to a can of beans and a thin slab of salted pork, and him with a wife and five children who all had mouths like baby birds needed feeding.

"You want, I'll finish yours for half," he said to Pablo.

"Sí."

The Mexican wasn't much on talking. Just walked over to his mule and rode off back toward town with Jim.

"I'll take the little gray filly and the dun," Jim said when they got there to the stable. "How much?"

The Mexican scratched under his straw sombrero as he calculated what he could get for the two horses.

"Maybe eighty dollars," he said after a few moments, saying it with a slight uncertainty, testing the buyer.

"Forty," Jim said.

The Mexican looked pained. Shook his head slowly.

"Seventy."

"Forty-five."

"Those two are my best *caballos*," he said. "Maybe sixty-five, but I don't know . . ."

"Fifty, and that's my final offer."

The Mexican shook his head.

"Oh no, señor, sixty is the lowest I could go."

"All right then, thanks for your time," Jim said and mounted the stud. "I guess I'll just have to find somebody else who wants to do a little business."

"There is no one," the Mexican said. Jim knew that already. Still, he'd set a price in his mind of fifty dollars and wasn't going to go beyond that.

"Maybe no, maybe yes," he said to the Mexican, and turned his horse away.

"Okay, señor, fifty dollars for the two . . ." then said something in Spanish under his breath Jim couldn't make out.

"It's a fair price," Jim said. "Put a rope on them and I'll go down to the bank and get your money and be right back."

The Mexican looked as though somebody had hit him across the toes with a hammer.

Jim rode to the bank, dismounted, and went in.

He waited his turn at one of the three teller windows. The windows had brass cage bars—the latest in security. Every teller kept a Colt pistol just below the counter next to his cash drawer. There was a big black steel vault in the back, a clock on the wall above the front door. At the far end of the cages was a small wood gate that led to the vault and area where the tellers stood, and a large oak desk with a swivel chair. It was a dry, quiet place with the feel of slow deliberateness to it. Hadley Prine was the bank president who sat at the desk where he could keep a keen eye on things and help out when the tellers needed a break for lunch or to go out back and smoke or use the privy.

Jim stood behind a woman with ginger sausage curls. She deposited twelve dollars and fifteen cents into her account, and the teller smiled broadly at her, his sprig of hair barely covering his otherwise bald pate. He wore a striped shirt with garters on the sleeves and a green eyeshade.

"Thank you, Glen," she said.

"Thank you, Polly," Glen replied, shyly as a deb-utante.

They both seemed reluctant to end the transac-tion, but finally the lady left and Jim stepped up to the window.

"Good day, Mr. Glass. Did you hear the terrible news?"

"I did. I'd like to withdraw seventy dollars from my account." Jim handed him his bank book—the one that showed he had a balance of eighty-three dollars and forty-seven cents.

Glen looked at it and said, "It won't leave you much in your account, Mr. Glass."

"I can cipher, Glen."

"Yes sir."

Hadley Prine looked up from his desk.

"Mr. Glass," he said.

"Mr. Prine."

Hadley wore garters on his sleeves too, but no eyeshade. His trousers were of a checked variety, and he looked overall like money.

"We've had some bloody business here in Domingo today."

"So I heard."

Prine shook his head.

"We shall never be a civilized town until the citizens are disarmed from carrying weapons so freely and men figure out a way to resolve their disputes without killing each other."

"You'll get no argument from me," Jim said. "But the way I heard it, it wasn't the citizens who did the killings, but a couple of strangers."

"True enough, but a complete ban on firearms might have saved us all such tragedy."

Jim waited for Glen to count out the seventy dollars.

"Make ten of that in silver," Jim said.

"Yes, sir."

Jim pocketed the money and his bank book with the new balance in it, and it just felt a lot lighter when he put it in his shirt pocket, but what couldn't be helped just couldn't be helped.

"Thanks," he said, and turned and walked out. The way old Hadley Prine had been looking at him was like he'd expected Jim to have done something about the shootings. Jim wished now it had never gotten out that he had once been a Ranger in Texas.

He rode up the street to Watson's Jewelry and dismounted again and went in. Hettie Watson, Bart's wife, pretty much ran things ever since Bart had fallen from a ladder when he was trying to shingle the second-story roof of their house and broke both legs and his pelvis. She was plump as a frying hen but with a quite pleasant nature. Jim could see old beauty hidden in her aged plumpness and imagined she was quite something when Bart had wed her.

"I come to look at rings," he said.

"What size do you wear?" she said with a cherubic grin.

He flushed.

"Not for me."

"A woman's ring, then," she said.

"Yes ma'am."

"Any particular type?"

"A wedding ring, I guess."

She looked at him with her round bright face.

"You're not sure?"

"I'm pretty sure—a wedding ring, yes."

She took a tray out of a locked metal box and set it on the counter. "These are some nice ones," she said.

"What about this one?" he said, picking out a simple band.

"Yes, that's a very nice one," she said. He looked at her knowing that it wasn't something she herself would have chosen.

"What would you recommend?"

"If it were me, I'd be impressed by this lovely gold band; see how it has the filigree work."

He thought it a handsome ring.

"How much?"

"This one would be forty dollars," she said.

He whistled low.

"I guess I'll have to look at something else.

"May I suggest something, Jim?"

"Ma'am."

"If you're only intending to marry once, then you might want to get the nicer ring—it will last longer than that thin silver one. Last a lifetime, I reckon, and look pretty on Luz's hand."

He flushed.

"How you know it's Luz I'm buying it for?"

"Jim, everybody in town knows about you and Luz keeping company. You ought to marry her. She's a fine woman."

"I'm not sure I'd care to hear what they're saying about us."

"It's not so bad what they're saying, if that's what concerns you. People will just naturally always talk, Jim. For my money, you two make a fine-looking couple, and she's going to absolutely love this ring."

"You sure enough ought to go into the horse trading business if you ever quit this line of work," he said. "You drive a hard bargain, but I just don't have the money."

"Tell you what. If you'd be willing to help Bart finish shingling the roof when he gets back on his feet, I could knock half off the ring; you can pay some now and the rest later when you get it. What do you think?"

"I'm sure not a roofer," he said. "But if Bart don't mind I'm not, then it's a deal."

"Okay," she said. "Let me just put it in a nice ring box."

"What if it's not the right size?"

"You tell Luz to come by whenever she wants and I'll have Bart size it."

"Kind of you," he said.

"I suppose you heard about the shooting?" she said as she dug through a drawer of ring boxes looking for the perfect one.

"I did."

"Real shame there's murder in our streets."

"Yes ma'am."

"Somebody should have done something. Trout was a good man and I reckon that old Tug Bailey was too, though I didn't know Tug all that well."

Jim didn't say anything but put the ten dollars on the counter and signed an IOU slip, saying he'd check in every once in a while to see how Bart was and bring her the rest of the money. Then he stepped outside again, the ring box in his pocket, mounted his horse, and rode back down to the stable, where he paid the Mexican fifty dollars for the horses, then led them by a lead rope at a walk before he put the stud into a gallop.

It wasn't any of his affair, he told himself—*what happened. Stay clear of it, Jim. You've got a peck of your own problems.*

He touched the ring box several times on his way back to the house.

Chapter Fifteen

El Paso, Texas

He had her bent over a barrel, her skirts hiked high, in a rain-washed alley while Willis waited his turn with her.

"Come on, now," he was saying, as though he were coaxing a mule to step over a log crawling with snakes. "Come on now, old gal . . ."

She was the lowest sort of whore—a crib girl without a crib to work out of since it had been torched a few days earlier by an irate and crazed self-appointed preacher. So she took men in the alleys or whatever handy shadow there might be, or behind some building, any place that wouldn't get her locked up by the local police; for they could be fearsome on whores with Albert Hightail as the new chief. He was a religious zealot, and perhaps the man behind the preacher's burning of her place.

The pious chief would just as soon see every whore run across the border and had already jailed her twice on charges of loitering and disorderly conduct. Her name was Alma Washburn and she'd left a husband and three kids back on an Iowa farm for what she thought would be a grand adventure after meeting a westbound rake who proved out to be an ex-convict who'd tossed her a line with his charm hooked on the end of it. She'd stolen the sugar bowl money as surely as he had stolen her heart, and together they took the noon flyer out of Sioux City. But he shook her off the hook there in El Paso and disappeared.

She had choices of course, as every single woman of her era did. She could scrub clothes for a Chinaman or sell what God gave her—something to that point, she reminded herself, she'd given away for free. She chose the latter because the money was at first quicker and a lot easier. She could do what she did and keep her eyes closed and her mind back on her children in Iowa, which is mostly the way she did it. But then came the pox and addiction to opium to help her get through life, and ten years later she found herself bent over a barrel of Hatch's choosing—not wanting to waste his hard-earned stolen cash on a room—there in the back of the Express Saloon and Billiards Parlor.

And while he was doing to her what it was men did, she thought of her children: they'd be grown now; Mattie eighteen and Roy nineteen. Sometimes she thought of Duck, her husband, wondered if he'd remarried, wondered if he ever thought about her. Most likely not, she told herself. And who could blame him?

"Come on now, gal. Come along there . . ."

She looked at the other one, waiting. Squirrel teeth when he grinned, yellow as acorns, a brush of whiskers on his chin reminded her of the mad preacher, fiery torch in his hand coming at her through the darkness. Both had real long faces and jug ears, and no doubt possessed.

"That's it, honey," she said in the same monotone repetition she used on every man to get him to hurry along, get it done and over with. "Give Angel the goods now, honey . . ." She called herself Angel because she felt like one that had fallen down into the mud, its wings tore loose.

Willis looked on eagerly as Hatch thumped into the woman, then gave a long, deep groan as though somebody was pulling his carrot out by the root. Hatch finally staggered back away from the woman, fumbling with his trousers that had fallen around his ankles into the mud.

The whole alley stank of the garbage of rotted food and urine that stained the walls of the buildings where the men went to relieve themselves of the ice beer.

"Your turn," Hatch said, and before he could even get fastened all the way up, Willis was humping her too. Hatch had lost his fever now and turned and walked to the head of the alley and rolled himself a smoke, thinking about the telegram in his shirt pocket—the one that had arrived earlier from guess who? He couldn't believe it. It was Cicero Pie, old Louisa's boy, the sister-in-law he'd humped that time he was back there. She'd told him the other one, the half-wit, Ardell, had seen the two of them. Shit, as if he cared.

But he must not have said anything to the hothead, Cicero, like she'd warned him not to, for Cicero had turned into a real mean son of a bitch from everything he'd heard about him since. They'd taken to calling him the Mortician because of all the bodies he'd left in his wake. Now he wanted him and Willis to come to Domingo and help them do a job there. The telegram didn't say what, because it was coded, he reckoned so the telegrapher wouldn't catch Cicero's meaning: *Come quick if you get this. Big job ready to go. Need two extra top hands. C. Pie. You remember me, don't you? Reply soon as possible.* Was postdated Domingo, New Mexico Territory.

He'd shown it to Willis.

"What do you think?"

"It ain't like we're making a fortune round here."

"I'm surprised to hear from that old boy."

"The way you did his maw, I guess so."

"She was ugly—never knew why John married her

to begin with till that afternoon when she showed me her talents."

They both stood grinning there in the middle of the rainy day, first rain either of them had seen for weeks.

"I guess we should go on up and see what the deal is."

"Why not?"

"Just thinking about it has got me all stirred up."

"Pulling a job, you mean?"

"No, how it was that day with John's wife."

"I'd like to have been there."

"I bet you would."

"How much we got between the two of us?"

"I got nine dollars and fifty cents, you?"

"Three dollars and this liberty dime."

"I say we get a little something to take the edge off."

They found Alma hanging out front of the saloon looking lusty-eyed, ready to conduct a little business. They'd bought a bottle they had with them and already half-drunk down.

"You boys hankering for a gal?"

"Yes we sure as hell are."

"Five each."

"How about fifty cents apiece."

She shook her head sadly, as though she pitied them or herself or the whole damn world for the sorry condition it was in. She used to get upward to twenty dollars a pitch. But she was running low on fuel these days, and a gal still had to eat.

"I get paid up front."

"Hell, here you go . . ."

So there she was now getting humped in the alley by the other one—the one with the yellow squirrel's teeth. Him just grunting and not even saying, "Come on old gal, come on." Working away like a man trying to chop down a tree.

Lucky for her he had a real hair trigger and finished in less than two minutes.

But in that flash of time, she was transported to a bed in an upper room of a new farmhouse painted white so that it stood out among the rolling green fields. The windows all open to let in the spring breezes that blew at sheer curtains and caressed her youthful naked skin better than any lover ever could, and knew that before the next morning she would take her life because she just couldn't go on doing life this way—bent over a barrel for fifty cents and letting bucktooth dirty strangers rut away inside her.

Willis came out to the head of the alley where Hatch stood smoking a cigarette, the rain that passed through earlier now fleeing east in a dark gray curtain with charcoal streaks, leaving behind great puddles in the street that reflected like hand mirrors.

"Something's wrong with her," he said.

Hatch didn't turn round to look.

"What?" he said.

"I don't know, she's just back there crying."

"You hurt her with that?"

Willis looked down.

"No, I don't reckon so. I mean I don't see how."

"You didn't bite her with them squirrel teeth did you, like she was a nut needed cracking open?"

Hatch was always making fun of his teeth.

"No, I didn't bite her."

They could hear her back there sobbing but didn't turn around or trouble themselves to go and check on her. She was, after all, just a whore.

"I say we go get some vittles and then buy a pair of tickets up to New Mexico."

"I guess we worked up an appetite, huh?"

"I'm about tired of this goddamn El Paso, ain't you?"

"Been tired of it since the second day we got here."

"Nothing here but Mexicans and gun artists. Too many damn policemen to suit my tastes."

They walked up the street to where their horses were tied in front of the hardware store but stopped and bought some tacos off a street vendor to eat along the way to the train station.

She had enough to buy a bottle of mercury. Enough to swallow and put an end to the memories of children and sweet rolling fields of grass and clover and

corn growing tall as a man by the Fourth of July; of
picnics and lemonade and harsh winters and lakes
frozen over thick with milk-colored ice; of a man
coming in smelling of cows he'd milked before day-
light and again before nightfall; of a good-looking
rake who stole then broke her heart easily as a hammer would a glass bowl; of weddings and baptisms
and funerals.

Yes, just one little bottle of mercury would put an
end to all those fine sweet memories just as quick
as it would put an end to the rough rutting of
smelly men and cold shivering nights under frayed
blankets in doorways; of dazed and forgettable
days without pleasure and the general molestation
of her soul.

*O, sing to me of they sweet sin and I will send
Jesus to save ye* . . . The mad preacher's words ring-
ing in her ears as he set blaze to her only refuge.

"We best go wash off our carrots before whatever
that whore may have give us gets down into our
blood," Hatch said, finishing the last of his tacos as
they sat there in front of the train station. "Woman
like that gives a man diseases will turn his brains to
worms."

"We could go down and warsh them in that creek
yonder," Willis said.

"That ain't no crick, that's the mighty Rio
Grande."

Drunk like they were with whiskey and the sense of power a man gets from taking a woman, they laughed like fools.

"I hope that job Cicero has in mind has lots of money attached to it."

"I never humped a woman for two bits before."

"I have. Once in Mexico. She didn't have no teeth."

"Maybe the women in Domingo is nicer."

"Let's hope."

"Life's about an interesting son of a bitch, ain't it?"

"Sure is."

Chapter Sixteen

The breed was there on the porch, hadn't moved, and Jim felt a sense of mild relief as he rode up and tied off the horses.

The breed studied them.

"Which one is mine?"

"Neither one, but you can ride the dun."

Jim stepped up on the porch and took the ten silver dollars from his pocket and held them forth. Hairy Legs's eyes glowed a little.

"My traveling money," he said. "Get me back East to see what that Free Love Society is all about."

"Yeah, good luck with that. Let me go inside and tell my woman I'm back," Jim said. "Then we'll get going."

"She's up there," the breed said, pointing to the ridge.

Jim saw Luz up there by the headstones. He walked up.

"What are you doing?" he said.

"Just looking."

"Got something for you."

She turned her gaze away from the headstones.

He took the ring box out and held it forth in the palm of his hand. She hesitated in taking it.

"You shouldn't have," she said.

"Go on and take it if you would. I think I might have done all right in picking it out." He was going to make a joke of it, tell her he had to nail on a roof for it, but decided the moment required a more serious approach.

She pushed herself against him, and he held her tight.

"You okay? That breed didn't try anything, did he?"

"No. I'm okay. I just want you to hold me for a moment."

They stayed like that for several seconds, then she leaned back and opened the hand that held the ring box.

"Are you sure about this?"

"As sure as I've ever been about anything."

She opened it slowly and he watched her face, her eyes as they settled on the ring. Then her gaze lifted to meet his own, and he could tell he'd done well.

"Put it on, see how it fits. Hettie Watson at the jeweler's said if it wasn't the right fit you could bring it by and Bart would fix it."

"You put it on for me."

"Okay, I will."

It was a little large for her slender fingers, but it didn't matter.

"I feel like your wife already."

"I feel like you are, too."

He kissed her then, her mouth warm and soft as ripe fruit.

"I could stay just like this forever," she said.

"You know I have to go with the breed."

"Yes."

"The sooner the better."

"Yes."

"I brought you something else," and he pointed down toward the house at the little gray filly. "I want you to ride home before it gets dark. Take the shotgun, just in case."

She looked worried. He told her not to be. They walked down the slope of the ridge together, arm in arm. The breed watched them from the far side of the dun, his arms resting across the animal's back. Dark woman, white man, didn't seem to quite fit. Made him envious that it did.

He waited while the man and woman went in the house and came back out again, and then waited some more while Jim saddled the horse for her and helped her into the saddle, then handed her up a shotgun.

"I'll come for you when we finish this business," he said.

She nodded, looked at the breed, then turned the horse's head toward the road to town.

"You ready?" Jim said.

"You?"

"Yeah, I'm ready. Lead out."

The breed rode the dun up the ridge, then down the other side to the bosque where he'd found the horse apples. He crossed the river where it riffled shallow over river stones, then walked the horse up and down stream till he was satisfied and punched his heels into the dun's flanks.

Jim followed, thought the breed kept a good seat for an Apache. But then he wasn't all Apache, was he? And he still wondered about that cavalry jacket, how he'd come by it.

They rode till the sun was nearly set beyond the Capitans, the rays split by the mountain's jaws. The breed pulled rein and got down. There was a pile of cold ashes under a scrim of dirty snow that lay in the lee of a big juniper.

"Made camp here," he said after closer examination of the ground, then looking off toward the southeast. "Two horses, two men, now."

"Looks like they're headed toward Domingo then."

"Looks like."

"Guess that's where we ought to head."

"Dark in half hour."

"I know the way."

"Fine, unless they turn off and go another direction before they get there."

"What are you suggesting?"

"Make camp here, start first light."

It made sense.

They built a small fire in the ashes of the old one using pieces of dry ocotillo they scouted until darkness fell over them like a purple blanket.

"Guess I should have thought to bring some supplies from the house," Jim said almost apologetically. Between what had happened earlier and his concern for Luz and buying her the ring and giving it to her, he'd plumb forgotten to think ahead; that finding the horse killer might take more than a day.

"We could shoot a crow if we saw one," Hairy Legs said.

"*If* we saw one."

Hairy Legs squatted in front of the fire, the light dancing in his leathery old face.

"I used to could conjure up crows and other creatures," he said.

"Why don't you conjure up a nice big fat rabbit or something then. I'd rather eat a rabbit than a crow any day."

"I would too. I can't conjure up no more."

"Why not?"

"I don't know. Just can't. Got to be too much like a Mexican, I guess it is."

"That's what you are, part Mexican?"

"Little Irish in there, too, somewhere."

"Irish?"

Hairy Legs shrugged. "I think so, way back on my mother's side."

"Interesting."

They sat and listened to the night sounds—the yip of a coyote, the coo and chuck of quail dusting themselves in the dark shadows, and at some point, the snort of javelinas rooting around in the scrub.

"Had some light to see by, we could shoot one of them pigs," Hairy Legs said.

"Be a waste of bullets with no light."

"Maybe one will walk into the light and let us have a look at him."

"Fat chance."

They lay down on the ground and did the best they could with sleeping. Hairy Legs had an easier time of it than Jim, who lay there staring up at the speckle of stars thinking about Luz. Where was she just now? In her bedroom brushing her hair, thinking of him?

He had never felt so tangled up over a woman before. Not like this. He told himself he wanted children. A son. A little girl. He wanted someone to carry on after he and Luz were gone. *It's the way it should be*, he told himself. *We don't come here just to disappear and leave no trace we ever been.*

"You asleep?" he said.

"Almost was, you hear something?"

"No, just wondering."

"Wondering what?"

"You believe in a life after this one?"

"Don't hardly believe in this one."

"What do you think happens to us when we die?"

"Somebody digs a hole and puts us in."

"You think that's it?"

"It's all I can figure."

"Don't think we have a spirit, or a soul, or whatever you call it?"

"My granddad believed in that stuff, but I never could conjure it. Seems to me this life is enough to conjure without thinking about some other."

"You afraid of dying."

"No, but I'd just as soon not be there when it happens."

Jim smiled to himself.

Me neither, he thought. *Me neither*.

Chapter Seventeen

It did not rain the day they buried Tug Bailey and Trout Threadneedle in the small cemetery outside Domingo. There was plenty of sunshine splashing the ground and a warm breeze blowing up from the river. It was, all in all, as pretty a day as anyone could wish for.

It was a short, slow ride from town to boneyard with both coffins in the same glass-sided Sayers and Scovill hearse pulled by Alfred Burpee's matching Morgans with their polished headstalls sporting black feathers. They were proud stepping horses, as though they understood the solemnity of their duty and were eager to perform it. Alfred Burpee sat up top, the reins threaded through his kid-gloved hands, wearing his best mourning suit and top hat. A fanciful man who accorded the dead their proper due. Next to him sat Melo, his protégé, a slight Mexican who always found funeral processions made his chest swell with a certain strange pride. To bear the dead to their final resting place was an honorable profession.

When the bodies had been brought into his mortuary, Alfred said to the boys who carried them, "When it rains it pours. First deaths we had around here in six weeks since old lady Brown. Lay Trout on the table and rest old Tug there on the floor till I can get to him."

The body bearers did not stick around. The copper embalming machine with its rubber tubes and steel needles, the shelf of cutting instruments, and bottles of strange liquids emitting even stranger odors were a sight none of them cared to dwell on. Simple truth was, he'd get them all, sooner or later—though not all would die of gunshot wounds like these two hombres. Some would simply die of age, and others of accidents. Some would die of disease, diphtheria or smallpox, or an infected tooth. But sooner or later, all would end up on his table, including himself and even the younger Melo and all Melo's family and so on and so forth.

He'd learned his trade in the war under a man named Holmes who had held an exclusive contract with the United States Army for embalming dead soldiers so that their bodies could be shipped home to their loved ones. Holmes was a wise and enterprising man who'd resigned his officer's commission, then went about the country selling families of soldiers embalming coupons. He placed advertisements in all the newspapers and hired a cadre of salesmen, and dozens of apprentices like Burpee, who would scour the battlefields after a fight looking for those lads with the coupons on their person. These would be taken and embalmed, packed in a lead or zinc-lined coffin, and shipped home.

Holmes showed him how to bleed out the corpse if it wasn't already, which many were from their grievous wounds. Showed how to cut an incision in the armpit to raise an artery and pump in a solution of bichloride of mercury or some other mixture to hold off decay for a "fairly reasonable amount of time." It was mean work, but work that needed doing—a kindness, in other words, to the grieving widows, maws and paws, back home.

Thing Alfred learned most of all, it was a trade that never lacked for business. As old Tom Holmes often expressed: "Everybody is one day or other going to require our service—there just never will come a time when they won't."

Embalming combined with undertaking services proved a modest living in a far-flung town like Domingo. But since Burpee's was the only game in town, he had a house bigger than the local physician's and almost as grand as the banker, Hadley Prine.

Trout was a boulder of a man, white as a bedsheet in death, except for neck and hands and face that were brown as sandalwood from years of sun and wind. It seemed impossible that a chunk of lead small as the tip of his little finger could kill a man so large. But it had and that's all there was to it. Alfred schooled Melo on bleeding the lawman out, letting the blood drain down the runnels of the enameled embalming table into a pipe drain that went into the ground he'd flush later with water. Then he used the copper embalming machine to pump a couple of gallons of Professor Rhodes Electro Bal Embalming Fluid into the late constable, powdered his face, waxed his mustaches, combed his hair, and had Melo help dress him in a suit of dark clothes split down the back and tucked under. Folded the arms and lifted him into one of Melo's handcrafted coffins they carried in from the shed out back.

Same thing with Tug—only a much lighter load to work with—all bones and ribs, thin papery skin white as bread flour, several old scars could have been caused by knives or bullets or both; a birthmark on one leg across the shinbone looked like a wine stain.

"Dress him in a boiled shirt and comb his hair, Melo." Melo, who crossed himself every time he worked with the dead—*los muertos*. Melo, with a fat wife and three happy children who depended on him to feed and clothe them and keep a roof over their heads. Melo, who made good coffins out of pine and stained them dark and gave them nice rope handles. Melo, who got three of the seven dollars Burpee charged for each coffin and three more dollars for each body he helped embalm, thought of himself as fortunate to be taught such a skillful trade. Burpee, with no kin, promised Melo someday he'd take over the business when Burpee himself passed, was obedient and patient in the waiting for that time to arrive.

"Sí, señor . . ."

By evening the corpses were ready for visitation, but no one came except for Little Paris, who arrived dressed in mourning clothes, like any proper widow might wear. Complete down to the hat with veil covering her face, black gloves. She sat in the parlor between the two coffins, looking from one still face to the other.

What fools, she thought. *To defend my honor when I have none.* She rose after a reasonable time, kissed the cold marbled foreheads of each man, then left to go and conduct her usual business as a bride of the multitudes. Life goes on. And though she would not get to sleep until nearly four that morning, she would rise before her usual hour to attend the funerals of the two men out of an abiding respect. The least, she told herself, she could do for those brave fools.

It was a grand funeral all in all, considering the two men had few true friends, but were the acquaintance of nearly everyone. Practically the entire populace turned out, not so much out of grief, or even respect, but for the spectacle of it. Like a wedding.

The town's little makeshift band, consisting

mostly of Mexican musicians, played their trumpets and strummed their guitars, and one man—Melo's cousin, Alberto, beat the bass drum all the way to the graveyard.

Father Zamora performed the services at the freshly dug graves, speaking in monotone about ashes going to ashes and dust to dust and walking through valleys of death without fear and so forth and so on. Then it was over and everyone drifted back toward town as the caskets were lowered by ropes held by Pablo and the Negro, Black Bob; Menlo and Alfred Burpee, their arm muscles straining against the dead weight. And once lowered, Pablo and Black Bob set to filling in the graves.

Ashes to ashes, dust to dust, life to death. No symbols of crows or rain or lightning from above, no ascending or descending doves or angels, just silence and drops of man sweat plopping into the dirt mounds as the thud of shoveled dirt struck down on the wood coffins.

Afterward Pablo and Black Bob sat and smoked in the shade of a chinaberry tree and drank from a bottle of Old Boot—an acidy whiskey that might have been fermented with, among other things, snakeheads—and smacked their lips as their sweat dried across their faces and in their shirts where it stained dark.

Having little in common except their trade as part-time grave diggers, they did not speak but smoked and drank in silence, then lay down in the dark shade and slept like the weary men they were, like men whose entire lives consisted of labor, like dead who had not been buried.

A dog with a shaggy gray ash-colored coat came up and licked their faces as Black Bob dreamed of a woman he'd known in the badlands when the law was still after him. A kindly woman with voodoo hair and voodoo eyes, a mulatto with skin the color of honey and breasts big as watermelons.

Oh, she had such a tender mouth, and in the dream he wore a silk hat and carried a silver-headed cane. The dog licked and licked at the sweaty face, then trotted off after lifting its leg against the tree, satisfied it had accomplished all there was to be accomplished here in this place of crosses and stones and sleeping men, both under and atop the ground.

Chapter Eighteen

In the morning they followed the tracks down to the road leading to Domingo. Here the tracks got mixed in with others traveling that same road.

"What do you think?" Jim said.

"Town," Hairy Legs said. "Big man like him gets hungry. No place else to eat."

"I agree."

Jim reined his horse.

"I guess I can go on alone from here," he said.

"Fine by me."

Jim looked at the horse Hairy Legs sat.

Hairy Legs started to dismount.

"No, it's okay. Keep the horse," Jim said.

Hairy Legs looked pleased by the gift.

"I promise not to eat him."

"I'm sure he'll appreciate it."

"Look for a big man walks funny."

"I will."

"Better look for the man with him too."

"I appreciate your help. Come round and visit sometime if you want and we'll drink a little of my whiskey."

"Your woman, she won't care?"

"No, I don't think so."

"Maybe I will."

"See you around."

"Okay."

Jim rode on toward town knowing what he was supposed to be looking for, hoping he'd find it. He didn't look back. Hairy Legs sat his horse watching the man ride. He didn't think he would want to be the big man or the one with him when this man caught up to them. It would be interesting to see what happened. Maybe he would just tag along to see.

But not too close, eh.

The streets of Domingo were quite still early as it was. The buildings on either side of the main drag looked sleepy and somber in the cold light of dawn. Jim decided to ride to Luz's and check on her, perhaps have some breakfast together. She lived just on the north edge of the town in a small brown adobe that sat behind an adobe wall.

He reined in and went through the gate and up the short stone path, where he knocked on the heavy wood door.

A hummingbird hovered near a small stand of

manzanita—its body iridescent green, its wings
thrumming the air. He thought hummingbirds were
a sign of good fortune.

He knocked again and waited.

Eventually the door swung open and there she
stood, sleepy-eyed, in a cotton shift, and when she
saw him, she threw herself against him, her arms
wrapping round his neck, and kissed him sweetly
on the mouth. He could feel the heat of her body
through the shift—it was like a warm fire on a cold
night.

"I dreamed of you," she said.

"What did you dream?"

She smiled.

"Come inside and I'll tell you."

He was once again amazed at his desire for her,
hers for him. They made the bedroom—barely.

Later they lay in the sharpening light of a fresh
sun crawling over the sill and sliding into the room,
spilling over the rich brown tiles.

"Did you find your man yet?"

"Not yet. I think he might be here in town."

"How will you know him?"

"He's traveling with another man. The one I'm
looking for is big, walks with a limp maybe, according to the breed."

"Speaking of the breed, where is he?"

"Left him up the road."

He felt glad to be with her, saw that she was still
wearing the ring.

"When do you want to get married?" he said.

"Soon."

"What about your children, have you told them yet?"

"They are with my *madre*, remember?"

"Yes. In Santa Fe?"

"Yes. I will tell them when they come home at the end of the week."

"Do you think they'll approve?"

"Yes. I know they like you."

"I like them too."

"Good, then we will all get along nicely." She laughed and squeezed herself against him.

"Careful, I'm an old man," he teased.

"Oh, not so old," she said, reaching under the blanket.

Hairy Legs sat his horse a short distance from the adobe. Sat there a long time, then turned its head around toward town and dismounted in front of the Dollar Café and went in.

There were only two other customers that early— a cattleman from Bosque Grande and his boy, a lanky kid with a shock of blond hair hanging out from under his hat. Both of them raised their gaze to meet the wild-looking breed.

Hairy Legs took a seat by the door, considered it an escape route, in case. In case what? He didn't know. Just in case.

The German's fat wife stared at him from behind

the counter, said something to her husband, who whispered, "Yah, yah, I see . . ."

Finally she came over.

"Vat you vant?"

"Eat."

"Eat?"

"Food," he said, making an eating motion with his free hand.

"Yah. Vat you vant?"

"Anything. Coffee too."

"You got der money?"

"Yah," he imitated and took the ten dollars from his pocket. She sniffed, said, "Okay, yah."

"Yah," he said again after she left; his ancient eyes hadn't seen wide, firm hips like that in a long time. It pleased him. Soft as lying on pillows, hips like that. Maria Armarillo had hips like that. He wondered if she was dead now. Could still see those dark smoldering eyes of hers in lamplight as the shadows danced over her—all that warm, waiting flesh. He liked his women big, real soft, something a man could settle into and stay that way comfortable.

The room smelled of warm breads, and it reminded him of his grandmother's fry bread, the honey she put on it. His belly growled.

The German's wife brought him sausages and scrambled eggs and coffee.

"Yah?" she said.

"Yah," he said.

"Seventy-five cents."

He pushed one of the silver dollars her way.

"Change please."

"Yah."

"Yah."

He watched her go off as he dug into the food. The eggs were bland but the sausages were tasty. The coffee was good and hot and dark tasting, like the earth. Good life, he thought. His mind wandered to the East. How long would it take him to get there, and once he got there, how would he find this society they called Free Love. Maybe find a woman with big, wide hips like the German's wife and take up with her. Fish every day and have her make him nice dark coffee and cook his sausages.

Then the door rattled open and a big man came in; a big man with an off gait who took up a chair at an empty table near the counter.

There's your horse killer, he thought. He kept a close eye on the big man, saw him hunch over his food like an eagle will do over a kill by spreading its wings. Little while later, a smaller man came in and joined him. Wearing a gun exposed on his hip, real bad-looking hombre. *There's your second man*. The German's wife came over holding the coffeepot, and Hairy Legs pushed his up forward for her to fill it, and in that instant, her gray eyes met his eyes, and some little secret passed between them. Her heated round face softened a bit, and she even half smiled as she filled his cup.

"Indan, yah?"

He nodded.

"Some of me, anyway. Mex too. Irish maybe."

She looked him over like a dog she was thinking of buying.

"You want to know which part's which?" he said.

"Yah," she said, after glancing over her shoulder back toward the kitchen where the German was sweating over the heat of a cookstove, several fry pans going.

"Yah," she said again. Those gray eyes twinkling now.

Maybe he wouldn't have to go all the way to the East.

She filled his cup with the steaming coffee.

"I live west of here," he said. "Up along the river. You just follow the river west, you understand?"

She nodded.

"I'm going there soon as I eat. Be there all day. Got plenty of room you want to come out. I'll show you something about us breeds . . ."

"Yah," she said, and turned back toward the kitchen.

He watched those big hips shifting like two fat coons fighting in a gunnysack and thought what pleasure they could provide a man who hadn't known any in a very long time. He stood after swallowing the last of the coffee and went out and got on his gift horse. Things were looking up.

* * *

There was a knock at the door. They were both dressed now, eating slices of pear and some coffee.

"Must be my day for visitors," she said.

"Must be."

She was more than a little surprised to see the breed standing there.

"He here, your man?"

"Yes."

Oh, those ravenous eyes sent chills through her.

"Jim," she called. "Jim."

He came to the door, saw the breed.

"Found your horse killer," he said.

"Where?"

"That place down the street—the eating place." Hairy Legs had never learned how to read, but so far in nearly seventy years, it had never been a problem. He could do just about everything else he needed to do. He'd been sent to school once when he was seven or eight years old, by his Mexican mother who insisted upon it. But it didn't take him long at sitting at a desk listening to chalk clacking on a blackboard while birds whistled outside to make his escape. He just leaped out the window and ran away.

"The Dollar Café?"

He shrugged.

"The other one's with him."

"You're sure it's them?"

"Big man favors one leg, smaller man wearing his gun out like he's ready to fight. You tell me."

Jim felt his chest go tight. He didn't doubt the breed for a moment, but proving these were the men who killed his horses, well, that might be another matter altogether. And without any law now to back his play, he'd have to play it just right. The other thing was, what was he going to do even if he could prove it was them, get one to confess to it? What was the right punishment except to ask for restitution—to ask them to get the hell out of town?

Well, there was only one way to find out, go and confront them and play it by ear, be ready to fight if he had to, but he sure didn't want to kill anybody over horses, but he wasn't just going to let them walk either.

"Thanks," he said to the breed.

Hairy Legs shrugged again and turned and walked back down the path and out the gate.

"Jim, don't go if there are two of them . . ."

"Got to, Luz. Can't let a man just come and destroy your property and do nothing about it."

"Then find someone to go with you."

"Who? Trout's dead. His deputies won't come out of their damn houses."

"Then I'll go with you."

"No," he said. "You will not."

"I know how to shoot the ten-gauge, remember?"

"I remember, but I'll not have you mixed up in this."

"If we're to be married," she said. "Then we're partners—in everything."

"No. Not this thing."

He went to the bedroom and picked his gun rig off the back of a chair where it had been hanging and shucked into it, settling the weight of the gun just under his left armpit, then put his coat on over it. Then his hat, and he stepped out into the main room again.

"Not to worry," he said. "I'm not aiming to let this get bloody."

"I don't want to be a widow again, this time even before I get married."

It caused him to smile.

"I promise not to let that happen."

He kissed her and went out, this time taking the ten-gauge with him from where she'd rested it just inside the front door. Just to make sure she wouldn't get any funny ideas about defending him, and just because it made a statement—the kind of statement even a blind man couldn't ignore.

The weight of his guns felt good, made up for the lack of help.

Set the odds back to even.

Chapter Nineteen

The half-wit was working on his second bowl of mush, spooning it in like no tomorrow. The Mortician sat across from him sipping coffee, a lit shuck between his fingers, the smoke curling up around his sharp-boned face.

"You eat like a hog," he said.

The half-wit's eyes flashed from the big spoon to his brother's.

"Why you have to say things like that?"

"'Cause they're true. Wipe your mouth, you got mush all over your mustaches. Looks like baby puke."

They heard the front door rattle open, close again, without paying much attention to it. The Mortician was thinking about the money in the bank—how much there was, would they be able to carry it all, even with Hatch and Willis?

"Tell you one goddamn thing, we get us a stake, you're on your own from now on."

"What you gone do, Cicero?"

"Get shed of this fucken country is what."

The half-wit looked suddenly glum as he spooned in the mush he'd been holding. He looked just like a big ol' baby is what he looked like.

Man's voice said, "I need to speak to you boys."

They looked up, saw a stranger, six feet tall maybe, gunfighter mustaches, hundred and eighty pounds that looked solid from where they sat. Saw too the heavy shotgun he was carrying.

"'Bout what?" the Mortician said. He was already feeling a certain tension.

"Why don't we go outside and talk." It wasn't a question; it was a suggestion.

"I know you?"

"No." The man looked at the half-wit brother. Cicero thinking, *This is some shit about those goddamn horses*. He wanted to reach across the table and bash the half-wit's brains in. Here he had lined up this bank job and fucken Ardell has to go and mess it up with some crazy-assed bullshit.

"Well, if I don't know you, I don't see as how we got anything to *talk* about."

"We do."

Ardell scarped the bottom of his bowl with the spoon, cleaning up the last little puddle of mush and honey. Then ate it and licked his lips and mustaches with a tongue looked like it belonged in a cow's mouth.

Cicero thinking, *Man, I sure don't want to blow this bank job by this goddamn fool's trouble.* He didn't look slow or old, this fellow. He looked like he could fight and would by the sound and sight of him. And what was that bulge under his coat up high but a fucken gun in a shoulder rig. Only one type of man kept a gun in a shoulder rig—a gunfighter. But it was the sight of that shotgun that troubled him most.

"Well, all right then," he said. "Sure, we'll take this outside if that's what you want. It don't make a shit where we talk. Come on, Ardell, let's go outside. This fellow wants to have a chat with us."

Then in she came, that little whore from yesterday, the one who got the old man and the lawman both killed over her. Come in and saw him right away and come marching across the goddamn room yelling at him, calling him ever' sort of a son of a bitch, letting Jim suddenly know just who he was dealing with.

He put out an arm as a barrier between Little Paris and the two men.

"You didn't have to kill them!" she screamed. "You didn't have to fucking kill them!"

"They started it, not me, you damn little tart."

"I've got business with these men," Jim said sternly.

She looked at him with the same furious eyes she'd looked at them.

"You're all sons a bitches," she said.

Jim nodded toward the door and held the woman off as the two men stepped toward it, Jim set to kill them both right there in the café if it came to that, if they forced his hand. He hoped they wouldn't force his hand. He said to Little Paris, "I need to deal with these men. After I'm finished, you want to keep cussing them out, that's up to you."

Then all three men were outside on the boards, sun splashing down in the street, Little Paris inside, furious and still cussing up a storm when the German's wife came over and tried to calm her.

"Please, please," she said. "Ve run a respectable business, fräulein . . ."

"Is that why you let murderers eat here, because it's such a respectable business?"

"No, no . . ." The German's wife had been pleasantly thinking about the breed, about when the breakfast crowd had finished coming in and before the lunch crowd started, telling Hans she was going to run an errand and take the buggy and . . .

Little Paris knew all her ranting was futile, that nobody understood or cared a goddamn about the dead. What's past is past, the living go on, things are forgotten, the memory of the dead is a meal eaten by time.

* * *

"So what is it you want to talk about, mister?"

"I think your friend here killed some horses of mine the other night," Jim said.

Cicero looked at the half-wit, feigning surprise.

"That true, Ardell, you kill this man's horses the other night."

There was a moment of hesitation. Cicero was about ready to let Ardell take the fall for his actions; he was sick of carrying the boy, his dumbness, like a child. Worse than a child. But he'd promised the old lady.

Ardell shook his head side to side.

"How'd you get that blood on your sleeves?"

Ardell looked at his still rolled-up sleeves. Where they bunched at his elbows they looked dyed reddish brown, like he'd soaked them in barn paint.

"Accident . . ."

"Look, we can settle this without a lot of heartache and grief," Jim said. "I'm willing to overlook the fact of what you've done if you'll pay me the damages." Jim knew the moment he saw the big man he was a half-wit, and as such, he knew it was possible that what may have possessed him to kill the horses was a question even the half-wit might not have the answer to. It was still an ugly goddamn act, but seeing the situation, he was willing to let it slide this time.

"How much payment you talking about here?" the Mortician said without any sincerity.

"Those were good horses, worth at least fifty

dollars each. Six of them, makes it three hundred dollars. That's about as fair as I can be on this."

"Three hundred, is that all?"

Jim wanted to smack the wise mouth.

"Yes, three hundred is what it comes to."

"Ardell, give this old boy three hundred dollars, would you, so we can get on with our day."

The half-wit patted his pockets, aping, grinning, flecks of porridge still stuck in his bushy mustaches.

"Nope, got no three hundred dollars. Sorry."

"That the way you want to play it?" Jim said. "Like this, like a fool?"

He'd left enough space between him and the two of them, three, four feet, but not too much. And when the smaller man tried to jerk his pistol, Jim swung the butt of the shotgun, striking him under the jaw and knocking him clear off his feet, then swung the ten-gauge round so fast, all the half-wit could do was stare down the twin muzzles like he was looking into the vacant eyes of death itself.

"You want to make it easy?" Jim said. "I could kill you both right here and now and nobody in this town would say one damn word because of that stunt you pulled yesterday. In fact, they might even pay me three hundred to rid the earth of you two . . ."

Cicero had misjudged his enemy, perhaps for the first time. He had still been tasting victory from killing those two fools yesterday. But now all he tasted was his own blood and the small, hard piece of tooth in his mouth that he spat out like a piece of corn.

The half-wit began blubbering.

"Go on, make it easy for me," Jim said.

"We ain't got no fucken three hundred dollars," the Mortician said, wiping his bloody mouth with the back of his hand.

"Where are your horses?"

"You gone steal our damn horses, you son of a bitch!"

"I'm going to get reparation for the loss of my property, one way or the other."

"Like hell!"

Jim set the hammers back on the shotgun. A crowd had gathered, formed a wide circle of citizenship around the scene, like a drama they'd paid good money to see, standing waiting with anticipation for the next act.

"What do you folks think I should do with these men?" he said.

At first nobody spoke, then a man shouted, "Do to them what they did to Trout and Tug Bailey. Don't give them no sort of chance." Then others chimed in. "Go on, shoot them no good sons a bitches. We don't want 'em around here!" This set up the chorus of cries for him to kill them—to rid the town of them, and it felt biblical to him, the way things were with the crowd calling for death and him with the power to deliver it.

It was a bloodletting wanting to happen. Then Jim saw Luz among the onlookers. Her eyes were sad, worried, her expression one of disappointment, and he knew he could not do it, that he should not do it.

"Anybody got the key to the jail?"

"I'll go get it," Woody shouted. He among them all, besides Luz, was the only one who had not called for murder.

After Jim had them locked away in the jail, he said to several of the men who'd tagged along, "Anyone want to volunteer to guard them?"

Nobody raised his hand except for Woody, the hotel clerk, the poet, the kid with eyeglasses.

"I'll do it."

Jim nodded and handed him the key.

"How long do I need to guard them?

"I don't know. I need to figure it out. Need to keep them in jail until we can get a judge down here to stand them trial."

"Should I have a gun, be armed?"

"You should." Jim handed him the shotgun. "You know how to use this?"

"I used to hunt geese with something similar back East."

"Same thing then. I need to find some more volunteers," Jim said. But nobody who'd followed them to the jail and stood there now in the small space made a move. He shook his head at such unwillingness.

He pushed his way outside to look for Luz, but she was gone from the crowd.

He went to the saloon, a gaggle of men trailing behind to see what he'd do next.

What he did next was ask for a cup of coffee.

Chapter Twenty

Jim stood alone while the others stood down along the bar watching him, telling Bilk what had happened. Bilk poured a cup of coffee and walked it down to the man.

"They say you took down those two killed Trout and Tug Bailey."

Jim did not answer.

"You know I'm also the mayor."

Still, Jim did not answer.

"We need us a new constable."

"I know that already. I wonder if you can tell me when the circuit judge is due in town next?"

"Week from tomorrow."

"You care anything about this town?"

"I'm here, ain't I, serving as mayor, running a business."

"Then use whatever powers you have to hire some men to guard that jail till the judge gets here."

"I'm offering you a job."

"Hell, I knew that yesterday."

"You did what they said you did with them two, you'd be the man I'd want as constable."

"I ain't looking for work."

"This something you think is beneath you?"

"No. I just got my mind on other things than kowtowing to drunks and breaking up fights."

"Seems to me you're out of business for the time being. Must be a good business, horses, for a man not to need no other kind of work."

Jim thought about his bank book balance; what was it, something like twelve, thirteen dollars now?

"Ain't nobody else in this burg willing to do it," Bilk said. "If there was, I'd already have hired them."

"Not interested."

"You just let those men kill your animals, ruin you like that, and you got nothing to say about it?"

"I did what I needed to do."

"You take the job you can hire you some deputies, can make sure those red dogs don't break out and kill some others of us. How long you think Woody's going to last standing guard? This town needs a take-charge man."

Jim sipped his coffee, recalled the look he'd seen on Luz's face as she stood in the crowd watching him—the deep disappointment, or was it sorrow, or was it something else?

"Look," Bilk said, softening his tone. "Tell you what, hire on till at least I can advertise and get me a steady man, till the judge gets here and holds a trial. I'll double the normal wages. Sixty dollars, and you can hire who you want to help you out with things till a new man comes. I'll put an ad in the newspapers in Santa Fe and Bosque Grande, should be able to get a new man in pretty shortly."

"I need to think it over."

"Sure, sure."

Jim took a nickel out to pay for the coffee; Bilk refused.

"It's on me."

"I'll be back to let you know."

"I ain't going nowhere."

Jim walked out wondering why he hadn't just turned Bilk down flat. Except sixty dollars was a lot of money for a week or so worth of work. He walked up to Luz's place, knocked on her door, and she let him in.

"You okay?"

"Yes," she said, still with that concerned look on her face.

"It couldn't be helped," he said. "What you saw out there on the street."

"I know."

"I gave them every opportunity to settle up with me."

She had a distant look in her eyes, like she was looking at something in her past. He knew she was looking at the corpse of her dead husband, laid out right here in the parlor of this house in a circle of lit candles, the light flickering on that handsome young face. He suspected she did not want to have to sit vigil for any more dead lovers, him included.

"It could have ended up a lot worse than it was," he said.

"What will you do now?"

"I've been offered to be the town constable until Bilk can hire a regular man."

"Is that something you want to do?"

"No, it isn't. I'm all about horses," he said. "But I'm down to pocket change in my bank account and it'll be some quick easy money; he's willing to pay me double till he gets a new man hired."

"And will that quick and easy money do you any good if those men, or others like them, come and kill you?"

He felt himself stiffen with old pride, pride a man like him always had, pride he couldn't just give up so easily.

"I have to do what I think needs doing, Luz. I can't change that part of me."

"I need to confess something to you."

"What is it?"

"When I returned yesterday, my heart was full of light and happiness, but I was also troubled too. So I went to see a woman I know who tells fortunes. I had her tell mine."

"What did she say?"

Luz's gaze lowered.

"She said a darkness approaches."

"I don't know what that's supposed to mean," Jim said. He had never been a believer in such things. Not before and not now.

"Let's find a priest to marry us."

"I want to wait until my children are home."

"Okay," he said

Hairy Legs had watched the man take the other two—the horse killer and the smaller one, saw how he handled them. Unafraid. Okay. Then rode to his place higher up the Pecos, a little money in his pocket, a good horse under him—not bad for not doing much.

He tied the horse good so it wouldn't run away, then went inside and found a bar of old yellow soap and walked down to the river with it, thinking of the German's big, wide-hipped wife.

He stripped out of his clothes and stood naked there at the river's edge, watching the brown flowing water move lazily along. The recent rain had made it run a little higher than usual. At its worst, it could be something to behold, overrunning its banks, carrying with it trees and coffins and bloated animals.

He waded in to his waist, the water cold enough to shrink his nuts, causing him to shiver. It had been seven months since he'd bathed last. It was time. He washed his hair and under his arms, his neck and

chest, his still strong legs made that way from years
of running as a youth. He was nearly as brown as
the river. Soap stung his eyes and he washed it out.
The water curled between his legs, and he thought
of the women he'd had in his lifetime. Gone now,
probably all dead or blind or crippled by time. He
remembered their beauty, and the memory had sus-
tained him over the years of living alone.

He rinsed off and came to the bank and took his
clothes and soaked them in the water, then scrubbed
them with the bar of soap and slapped them on a
big flat rock and rinsed them again and climbed out
carrying the wet clothing. He hung the clothes, still
dripping river water, from the lower limbs of a light-
ning-struck cottonwood and went inside the house
and found an old but clean blanket and wrapped
that around his shoulders and went back out again
and sat in the sun. The sun's heat took a long time
to get down to his chilled bones but finally it did,
and he felt better. He sat until the sun dried his hair
too.

He closed his eyes and dozed like an old dog and
was awakened by the sound of something strange.
And when he opened his eyes and looked there she
was—the German's big wife getting down from a
buggy had a leather quarter-top and was drawn by
a single roan horse.

She looked around at the place in a sort of wonderment.

"Yah," she said.

"Yah," he said.

"Yah, yah . . ."

He followed her inside the house. He pinched her big bottom, and she yipped. It was going to be a good day all the way around.

Jim walked back up to the Cat's Paw. The place had cleared out some, just one table of poker players, a couple of men standing at the bar jawing at each other. Bilk was looking at the cover of the ten-cent romance even though he couldn't read a word.

"I'll take the job," Jim said.

"I run it past the rest of the town council already and they approved."

"Got a piece of paper and a pencil?"

"Sure, somewhere."

"Get them."

Bilk went down the hall to the back, then returned with said items, and Jim wrote out a contract:

I, Jim Glass, do hereby accept the position of town constable for the town of Domingo in the territory of New Mexico on this day, April 9th, 1885, for the sum of sixty dollars for a period of not more than thirty days, or until a new constable is hired, but not longer than for a period of one month from this date. The amount will be paid in full to me . . .

Jim paused and allowed one possible consideration to enter his thoughts, then continued:

> *. . . or to be paid to Luz Otero in the event of my death. Further, it is agreed that any expenses I incur in the pursuit of my duties as constable shall be reimbursed to me by the town council including mileage.*
> *Signed: J. Glass.*

He left room for Bilk to sign it. Bilk looked slightly embarrassed when Jim handed him the paper and told him to read it and sign it.

"I never learned how to read."

Jim read it to him.

"Just make your mark there next to my name," Jim said, pointing to where. Bilk put an X and Jim wrote Bilk's name next to it, then folded the paper and put it in his pocket, intending to give it to Luz.

Jim went out again and walked to the jail where Woody sat the chair behind the desk in the small anteroom, the shotgun resting atop the desk.

"You want to be a deputy?"

"I've no experience."

"Neither did I the first job I took," Jim said. "Thing is if you think it beats clerking at the hotel."

"Not sure that it does."

"Fine, I'll find somebody else."

"No. I mean, well, I'd like to give it a try."

"Then I deputize you and see that you get thirty a

month. You know anybody else who has any grit to them would want to also be deputized?"

The name that popped immediately into mind was Black Bob.

"He picks up what work he can, digging graves, hauling freight between here and Lincoln, but I don't believe he has nothing steady. I think he'd make a good man for you."

"Where's he live?"

"Just south of town, quarter of a mile. Little hard-scrabble place with lots of chickens, some goats, a few pigs, lots of kids."

"Okay. You need relief, walk up and get you a beer and something to eat at the Cat's Paw, tell Bilk to put it on the tab, that you're my new deputy. I'll wait here."

Woody high-stepped it up the street, thinking this would be an adventure he would someday write about—that a poet's life was not one to be lived within four safe and boring walls, sitting behind a desk and handing people room keys, but out on the streets of the living humanity, the good and the bad—the blessed and the evil.

Jim went back to the single cell to check on his prisoners. They were there, one bleeding, holding his mouth, and the other looking befuddled. They looked at him with crusted hateful eyes.

When Woody returned, Jim instructed him at the noon hour to go and get the prisoners some sand-wiches wrapped in butcher's paper and a canteen of water and pass it to them through the barred opening at the bottom of the door, but not to unlock it.

Then he rode off south in search of Black Bob's place.

He spotted it right off, set back a dozen yards from the road. Could smell the pig stink because the wind was right.

Seven black faces looked at him when he rode up—the man's, the woman's, and the five children's, none taller than the man's waist. An old hound stood its ground, barking, its hackles raised. The chickens squawked like they were being murdered.

"Black Bob? That's your name, isn't it?"

"Robert Lee Washington," the man said.

"You looking for a job?"

"Always looking for a job, what you got needs doing?"

There was a buckboard in the yard, a pair of horses grazing from picket ropes. The house looked too small for all of them in it at one time. The red handle of a water pump stood waiting for someone to jack it. The woman was thin, had her hair bundled in a gray scarf. The kids—three boys and two girls—were barefoot, their clothes faded from wear and wash.

"I need another deputy."

"You the new law?"

"I am, for now. Name's Jim Glass." Jim extended his hand while sitting his horse, and the man came and shook it with a strong grip.

"You mean you want me to wear a gun?"

"Only if you feel comfortable wearing one, but yes, that's what lawmen generally do, wear a side-arm."

"Might rile some folks, black man wearing a gun, being the law over them."

"You let me worry about that."

"Might I ask what you're paying?"

"Thirty a month, same as the other deputy's getting. Thing is, I'm only temporary till they can find a permanent man. He comes, he might want to hire his own men, and you could be out of a job. But till then, the pay's a dollar a day plus meals, but a guaranteed month's worth of work no matter."

"Where do I sign up?"

"Raise your right hand and swear to uphold the law of the town of Domingo."

"I do."

"You got a gun?"

"Rifle."

"That'll do for now. Hie on over to the jail and relieve Woody come about six o'clock. I'll relieve you later on tonight."

"That's it then?"

"That's it."

"Yes sir."

"I'll let the others in town know what the arrangement is, but anybody gives you trouble, you come see me at the Cat's Paw. You know Bilk, the owner?"

"Yes sir."

"I'm not there, you ask him where I am."

"Yes sir."

"I'll see you later then."

Jim turned his horse back toward town. It was probably going to be a long week waiting for the circuit judge to arrive. But it was a thing that needed doing, and a week was only a week in a lifetime waiting for him.

He stopped at the mercantile and went in and asked to see a catalog had suits in it. Found one he liked.

"How's this work?" he asked Ortega, the owner. "I just order it, or what?"

"First we measure you."

Ortega measured him with a tape and wrote the numbers down on a slip of paper. The suit was fifteen dollars. It was a nice suit of black broadcloth, coat and trousers. Fitting enough for a man to be married in. Wedding suit.

Suddenly he felt different.

A good feeling it was too.

Chapter Twenty-One

They sat there over supper, across from each other in Luz's kitchen of Mexican tile, the big heavy wood table and chairs taking up most of the room. They'd eaten bowls of chili, warm biscuits. And now they sat smoking cigarettes and sipping whiskey.

"I ordered a wedding suit," he said. "A black one."

Her eyes seemed to brighten slightly, then dimmed again. She was thinking: *Wedding, or funeral?*

"Everything will be okay," he tried again reassuring her.

"Yes, of course it will."

They heard a bird singing outside; they weren't sure which kind. It was Saturday. People would be gathering for a dance in the plaza. In the quiet evening air they could hear the musicians tuning their guitars, practicing with their voices. Lights were starting to come on in the growing dusk, luminaries lit.

"I need to go check on the jail," he said.

She didn't say anything. Perhaps she'd drunk a little too much. Her features were loose.

"I'll come back in a little while and maybe we can walk down to the plaza, perhaps dance if you like. I'm not very clever with my feet."

He could tell she was filled with sorrow. He gathered his hat and settled it on his head and went to the door without any more conversation.

Went down the stone path to the gate, out it to the street. Looking one way he could see the flickering luminaries in the plaza, circling it, a glowing ring of flickering desire. The church just beyond stood sentinel like some moral overseer. He turned away and headed toward the center of town instead and to the jail where Black Bob sat, but choosing to sit out of doors to hear the music rather than within—the shotgun laid across his legs.

"How is everything?" Jim said.

"Fine, boss."

"Woody feed those men earlier?"

"Said he did."

"I want you to go get some supper, and bring them something too." Gave Bob the same warning he had given Woody—to slide the food under the barred door, not unlock it.

"Okay, boss."

"I'll wait for you to return."

Black Bob stood and headed up the street to the Dollar Café. Jim rolled himself a shuck and struck a match off the stone wall, causing a flame to jump to life, then put the end of his shuck to it and drew deeply before snapping out the match.

"Hey you son of a bitch, when we going to eat in here?" a voice shouted from inside. He knew it was the smaller man—the one called himself the Mortician.

He stood and went inside and looked at the two of them.

"Food will be here soon, hold your water."

"You got no right to hold us."

"Yeah, I do."

"I killed the goddamn lawman yesterday because he stuck his nose in my business and I'll sure as hell do the same with you."

"That was yesterday, and I'm not him, and you're locked down case you hadn't noticed."

"Then I'll by God kill you tomorrow."

"You're about a funny son of a bitch. Good luck with that, eh."

"Listen, you let us out, I'll give you the three hundred, even though we didn't have nothing to do with your horses."

"Stick the money through the bars."

Moment of silence like a paused heartbeat. Jim exhaled a stream of smoke.

"I'll have to go get it . . ."

"Yeah, good luck with that too."

Jim went out again and leaned against the wall and stared up into the deepening purple sky. People were starting to come up the street in earnest now, headed for the plaza, knowing the dance would soon begin. Two that wouldn't be there and would not be coming were old Tug Bailey and Trout Threadneedle. No more dances for them, ever.

After a time Black Bob returned carrying two pails. One held a stew, the other ice beer.

"Those aren't going to fit between the bars," Jim said.

Bob looked consternated.

Jim walked back inside with him and took the key from his pocket and called in.

"I'm unlocking this door so you boys can be fed, but you come out of there like caged badgers, the only thing you'll end up eating is lead and dirt. Stay back away from the door."

Jim unlocked the brass lock and unhooked it, then stepped back with the shotgun at the ready, nodded, and Bob set the pails inside the door, then closed the door and snapped the lock back into place.

"Have at it, boys," Jim said. Then to Bob: "You get yourself fed?"

"Yes, boss."

"Good, I'll send Woody around to relieve you later."

Black Bob sat alone, his chair tilted back against the wall outside, and listened as the music down at the plaza began to take hold of the night. It was sweet, heart-beating music that set one foot to tapping against the flatboards of the sidewalk. Oh, what he wouldn't give for his days of youth back. What a rover he had been, everything from driving cattle up the long lonesome to being a buffalo soldier with the Ninth. There were all sorts of gals, from high yaller to dark as coal, pretty gals and not so pretty gals. He loved the laughter of a pretty gal and wished he was out there in that plaza dancing with one now. Then he thought of his wife, how sullen and difficult she'd grown over the years from the sweet and meek gal she was when he took up with her. Now she was all loud mouth, full of bitterness, at whatnot, he didn't even know exactly. But he loved his children and knew he'd never leave her because of them. Oh, that music was surely sweet.

Later, after the music quit and the people had all gone home, Woody arrived, carrying a pistol in the waistband of his trousers, holding a lantern that swung light in the darkness.

"Bob, how you making out?"

"Good enough, you?"

"Good enough. Any problems with those galoots?"

"What sort of problem is a man locked up bound to give?"

"Don't know. None, I suppose."

"You come to relieve me?"

"Yes. You want a taste of this before you go?"

Woody took a bottle out of his back pocket and held it forth. It was blackberry brandy.

"Something to warm you."

"Thanks, boss."

Woody squatted on his heels and the two men passed the bottle between them, drinking slow, deliberate little mouthfuls of the sweet alcohol.

"You can go on home you want to," Woody said.

"Nah, it's okay, boss. Late as it is, all my kin will be in bed asleep."

"Should have brought a deck of cards."

"You hear that music earlier?"

"Yeah, I went down there to the dance."

"You do any dancing?"

"Some. Danced with a pretty little thing, but her mean-eyed mama kept watching us."

"Otherwise you'd danced off in the dark with her."

"I sure would have, I do believe."

"They tells me you write poetry."

"Yes, but it must not be very good. Can't get anybody to publish it."

"Don't mean it's no good."

"What good are words written on a page if nobody reads them?"

"Got a point there. Here's your bottle, boss."

"You ever read any poetry, Bob?"

"Can't say as I have. No time for such things as reading, too busy just trying to put a little meat on the table. Them kids of mine eat like they got no bottom to 'em, Alberta too."

Woody smiled in the shadow of the ring of light

thrown off by the lantern and bit off another swallow of the brandy, sloshed what little was left around in the bottom, and handed it back to Bob.

"No, boss, your liquor."

"Go ahead," Woody said. "I got to stay awake till dawn."

"Seems foolish to have us just sitting out here like this all night. Those two jakes ain't going nowhere 'less they can claw their way through these here walls with their fingernails."

"I know it."

Bob drained the bottom of the bottle, the liquor warming his blood and making him feel like he could tip over if he wasn't careful.

"I guess I best get on home," he said.

"Pleasure talking with you, Bob."

"Sure enough, boss."

"Hey, Bob."

"What?"

"You're walking the wrong way."

"I know it."

Bob had set himself a course for town. Maybe Little Paris would give him a throw on credit—against money he was about to earn end of the month. He felt lonesome for a loving woman, one wouldn't give him grief about every damn little thing in this old life. The liquor and music down in his blood now, running hot and to every part of his body, needed cooling off. Just a little, lawd. Just a little, as he walked off into the night.

Chapter Twenty-Two

Bilk heard the train's whistle a mile out yet. Next to him in the bed, the thing he'd wanted most since the first time he laid eyes on her—Little Paris. Drunk and snoring a low, steady snore that came and went with each breath. Still, he thought, in the midmorning light she was the most beautiful woman he'd ever seen, and definitely the most beautiful he'd ever lain with. She had one dark mole in the low center of her back, just above the swell of her hips like a single drop of India ink. What had surprised him most about her, other than the fact she'd knocked on his door in the middle of the night, after he'd gone to bed and let his hired man, Green, take over the running of the bar, was the size of her breasts. They were a lot larger than he'd thought they would be, and for such a small woman. They drank and he stared and she finally said, "Is that all you intend on doing, staring at my bosoms?"

Morning flyer, he thought when he heard the train's whistle. How often he'd thought about that train, where it would take him if he ever decided to climb aboard and say, *Take me far as you're headed*, and pay the fare and get off at that very last stop and start all over again.

The death of Trout had had a greater effect on him than he could have ever imagined. He always imagined Trout's disappearance from the scene would be a reason to celebrate—that without Trout around, he'd have a greater chance with Little Paris, who seemed to favor Trout over all the other men in the town, even though she didn't seem to favor any man overly much, Trout was the one who most often paid her visits.

But Trout's death left a dark hole of doubt in Bilk's own heart. For, if a man of Trout's gristle could be done in by a stranger's bullet, then everyone was susceptible, and death was always just around the corner.

"You okay?" he'd asked Little Paris when he'd opened the door to her knock and saw her standing there swaying like a snake about ready to strike.

"I'm just real sad, Bilk. Sad and angry at life and this grubby little town. Can I come in?" It was plain to see she'd been drinking heavily; she smelled like a whiskey bottle and could barely stand upright.

"Of course," he'd said.

"You got anything to drink?" she said, sitting on the edge of the bed.

"I'll run up front and get us a bottle."

"Of the best stuff . . ."

"Yes, of course, nothing but the best for you."

He came back and she was lying on the bed in just her chemise and stockings, and he thought, *My, my, this sure can't be happening to me.* But indeed it was.

They drank from the best bottle of champagne he kept stocked, drank it out of fluted glasses he'd kept for special occasions, ones he'd ordered all the way from New York. There had yet to be such a special occasion, but now there was.

She told him how she was sick to death of life the way it was, had more than once thought about loading her pockets with rocks and jumping into the river.

He didn't understand why a woman with her looks would ever want to do a thing like that.

"You just don't understand, Bilk," she said. "A woman's beauty can be her curse."

No, he didn't understand, but he took her word for it.

"I need to get out of this place, Bilk. I need to get gone. I can't live like this no more, dealing with drunks and cowboys and any old fool who comes along with the price of a fuck in his pocket."

"But that's what you do, honey. It's your stock and trade . . ."

Oh, she gave him such a look he felt shriveled inside. Shook her head sadly and said, "You see, nobody understands what it's like, being a whore, to be stuck inside myself with no other assets than my looks. And how long do you suppose a woman keeps her beauty, Bilk? And what happens after her beauty is faded to nothing and not even the buzzards want her?"

Well, he offered up his own brand of wisdom, but it was like a schoolboy trying to teach his teacher how to do mathematics or Greek philosophy when he himself didn't have a clue.

They drank down the one bottle and Bilk went and got another and they drank most of that, all the while Bilk doing his best to convince her things would be okay, that life had a way of working out, that she'd find her true path, that a rich man would come along and take note of her beauty and offer to marry her.

"Course it will be a sad goddamn day for me when that day comes, Paris, because I have been in love with you from day one . . ." There, he said what he'd long felt and was afraid to say to her. The champagne had loosed his tongue, maybe stolen his good sense too. The champagne and the sensual way she was posed there on the bed—without trying to be sensual, he guessed.

"You truly love me, Bilk?"

"I do."

"Then take me the hell out of this grub hole—take me to San Francisco."

"We can get married in the morning," he said.

"Married?"

"Yes, that's what you want, ain't it?"

"Oh, hell, Bilk. Oh, hell . . ." Then she'd passed out cold and he wasn't sure whether to take advantage of her in that condition or not. For there it was, the very object of his desire with nothing to stop him but his own sense of propriety; he didn't think he had any, but he did. He convinced himself that no matter how much he wanted her, he wanted her to be in love with him and to offer herself without any stipulations, such as money attached to the deal. He walked and paced the floor, telling himself he would not screw a passed-out woman, that he would wait for her to awaken—to be a true gentleman about it. To see how she felt toward him when she was alert and sober.

And thus he fell asleep next to his beloved only to be awakened midmorning by the distant cry of the train's whistle. Looked at the watch he took from his trousers lying there on the floor. Quarter till eleven. Train was fifteen minutes late. Everything in life seemed to be off kilter since the killings.

He swung his bony legs out of the bed and sat there on the side, his head held in the cups of his hands. He tried hard convincing himself that this was the way it should be—him waking up every morning with Little Paris there in the bed with him. A life of rising late and going to the café for a late breakfast, then strolling the streets of San Francisco or some other notorious city together, of going to museums and to the ocean, dressed in swell clothes and being this handsome couple who got invited to wealthy parties—the frontier dust shook off their shoes forever. Maybe even have a couple of youngsters. But in fact, he knew such a future was as unlikely as it was for him to be struck by lightning while riding a wild buffalo and holding a rattlesnake in his teeth.

He put on his trousers and stepped into his shoes and laced them, then stood and looked down at his pretend wife, the small knob of one bare shoulder exposed, and leaned over and kissed it. She hardly stirred.

Two men stepped off the train, then walked toward the rear where the stock car that held their horses shuddered and waited for one of the railroad men to come and open the door and slide a gangplank into place. They stood there smoking, looking around at the collection of buildings, toward the wide main drag.

"Quite a little shithole, ain't it?" Hatch said.

"Sure the hell is. I hope whatever damn job old Cicero has in mind is worth it. I'd hate to have come all this way for nothing," Willis said. "What'd them tickets cost us, six dollars?"

"You remember to keep your mouth shut about what I told you about me and his old lady, you hear? He even gets a whiff of that and somebody's going to end up dead."

"I still can't believe you horned her. Old woman like that, and your own sister-in-law to boot."

"She ain't no older than me and being kin don't have a thing to do with it. Fact, it made it even more interesting she was."

"Still . . ."

They waited till their horses got led down and handed to them, the railroad man gruff in gray overalls, hair thick as a brush, face looked like it was squashed in by something in the long ago.

They mounted and rode their horses up through town via the main drag, taking in the business establishments as they went; the big stone bank on the corner looked especially inviting.

"You think that's it?" Willis said. "You think that's what old Cicero got us up here for?" Hatch shrugged. They saw the Cat's Paw farther on and reined in; though it was not yet even noon, both men craved a drink. To hell with coffee or breakfast first.

"Get us a drink and ask around about Cicero and the half-wit, Ardell," Hatch said.

They dismounted and went in and walked to the bar a minute after Bilk had come and relieved his man, Green—telling him to get to cleaning up the place, then setting a pot of Arbuckle to boil on the stove.

Two customers already, but he wasn't truly interested in business this day. He kept thinking about Little Paris back there in his room, how maybe he shouldn't have been such a gentleman after all, because the buzzing in his blood wouldn't let up.

"We're looking for two old boys," Hatch said after he ordered them each a short whiskey and Bilk had poured it and taken their money from the wood.

"Who might that be?"

"Little fellow and a big half-wit boy. Think maybe they hit town not too long ago."

"Why you looking for 'em?"

"It's sort of personal business," Hatch said.

"Well, you're going to have to go and talk to Constable Glass about that, mister. He's got those boys locked up."

Well, there was a piece of unexpected news. Hatch and Willis exchanged looks.

"What they in the jug for?" Willis said.

Bilk held the bottle aloft and said, "You boys want another short one?"

"Sure," Hatch said. "It ain't that early."

Bilk poured, and it was Willis's turn to pay the freight, and he put two more bits on the wood.

"Murdering horses," Bilk said.

"Murdering horses?"

"Constable says they murdered his horses, come in the middle of the night and did it." Bilk shook his head trying to get the erotic buzz out, feeling the need to distract himself from thoughts of naked whores in his bed.

"Funny," Bilk continued without being asked to

elaborate. "But here that one, the little fellow, shot down the other constable we used to have and another fellow, right out there in the street—in front of the hotel. It was a goddamn sorry thing to do, but all perfectly legal according to the law because it wasn't the little fellow who started it. Now here they are in the jug for killing a man's horses. Just goes to show you no bad deed goes unpunished."

"You got some screwy damn laws round here," Hatch said, smiling.

"It is what it is."

"Where's the jailhouse?"

"Up the street across from the undertaker's."

"Thankee."

Jim came eight that morning and relieved Woody, told him to go find Bob and tell him to come in, then fed the prisoners with food he brought from the Dollar Café—biscuits and fried ham. Marched them to the privy out back, then locked them in again. Both men cursing him, especially the smaller one.

"You can count on me blowing your brains out," he'd said on the march back from the privy.

"I'll make sure and remember that," Jim said.

"You make sure you do."

Jim went to the anteroom and sat down at the desk and rolled himself a shuck and smoked it waiting for Bob. But what he didn't know was Bob was down in bed, kicked in the chest by a horse he was trying to shoe for a neighbor. Broke several ribs, Woody reported when he returned, looking bleary-eyed.

"You go and get some rest and come back in a few hours," Jim said. Woody was yawning, tired from the all-night vigil. Sitting, trying to catnap in a chair while two snoring men slept like children, wasn't exactly how he'd pictured lawman work. Maybe it would get more exciting, he told himself as he headed for his room at the hotel.

Jim sat there thinking about Luz when the door rattled open and two men walked in. Lowbrow men from the looks of them, not from around this area.

"Here you got some relatives of mine locked up," Hatch said.

Jim stood, his coat off so the men could easily see the revolver in his shoulder holster, show them he was armed.

"I've got two men locked up, yes."

"How much to go their bail?"

"No bail's been set yet. Have to wait for the circuit judge."

"When you think that's going to be?"

"End of the week."

"You mind we have a word with them?"

"Put your sidearms on the desk and you can have a regular hymn singing if you want."

Hatch looked round to Willis and smiled and said, "Sure," and they pulled their revolvers and set them on the desk, and Jim walked them back.

"Talk away," he said.

"You mind if we speak private with them?"

"I do."

The half-wit saw Hatch and Willis, and right away the image of Hatch and his maw jumped into his mind like a flame come to life in dry tinder, and that was all he could think about—Hatch and his maw.

"Boys, I see you done got in a bit of a pickle," Hatch said.

Cicero came up to the bars slow, wrapped his hands around them like they were skinny necks he wanted to choke.

"You need to bail us out of here, we ain't done nothing."

"The constable here says no bail's been set, I guess there ain't nothing we can do but wait."

The two of them sent messages back and forth with their eyes, Hatch telling Cicero, *Don't worry about it, we got this thing in hand, just be patient.* Cicero warning Hatch he had better.

"Well, hell, I don't know why you all came if it ain't to help your poor old nephews out of a pickle. You got any tobacco on you?"

Hatch looked at Jim.

"It okay if I pass him my makings?"

Jim nodded. The makings were passed.

Guilty as hell, both of them, too dumb to stay out of jail. Killed some damn horses. What the hell would they even do that for? Jesus Christ, thought Hatch.

"Anything else you're needing I can get you?" he said.

"Just out of here," Cicero said.

"Rhubarb pie," said the half-wit.

Again that silent message with the eyes of men related by blood, kin to kin, and Hatch thinking, *The old lady had us both, me and my brother, and look what it's all come down to.*

"See you around, boys," Hatch said, and he and Willis marched back out again and asked for the sidearms.

"When you leave town, I'll give them to you," Jim said.

Anger like a piece of swallowed sharp glass stuck in Hatch and Willis's craws.

"You got no right."

Jim reached in the top desk drawer and took out the badge Trout had been wearing when he was shot, a speck of dried blood still on one point of star, and set it down on the desk like it was a piece of jewelry they might be interested in purchasing.

"This gives me the right."

"Gives you no goddamn—" Willis started to say, but before he got all the words out, Jim drew his pistol and cocked it.

"You want to see how I enforce the law?"

"It's okay, Willis," Hatch said, knowing they were as licked as Sunday ice cream this time around.

"We don't need guns while we're visiting. Looks like the constable here has everything well in hand. Let's go."

Outside Willis said, "You just going to let that son of a bitch take our guns?"

"Look up the street and tell me what you see."

"Nothing."

"Look again."

"See that bank, a dentist's office, a store . . . what the hell am I supposed to be looking for?"

"You think maybe they sell guns at that mercantile?"

Willis said, "Shit, Hatch, I should have known you'd have a plan."

Chapter Twenty-Three

She dreamed of horses. That the two of them were riding horses across the benchlands, the wind in their faces, the horses running so fast it was almost as if they were flying.

They came to a small blue-green pool surrounded by trees that spread their shade upon the ground, and there was a table full of food waiting for them. There were bowls of fruit and all sorts of meats, breads, wine.

And sitting at one end of the table was Hector dressed in a fine black suit, snowy white shirt, his hair combed and his eyes bright with anticipation.

He looked happily at her and said, "Who is your new friend?"

She didn't know how to explain about Jim.

They sat down to eat with Hector passing plates of food to them as the horses grazed by the pool on rich grasses, their beautiful forms reflected in the water, perfect mirrored images.

"I have been away," Hector said at one point. "But now I'm back."

And she felt suddenly and very deeply sad. For now she was caught between her love for both men but knew she could not keep them both—that she had to choose one over the other.

She asked, "Where did you go, Hector?"

He smiled, and she noticed that he did not touch a single thing on his plate that was piled high with food.

"Who is this man?" he suddenly demanded, his pleasant manner now charged with anger.

"He is my friend," she said in defense.

Then Jim suddenly stood and pulled his gun and shot Hector through the heart, a bloom of red flowering in the white shirt. In the dream she cried, she wept with sadness.

She awoke to find her bed empty and realized she'd had a bad dream.

She dressed and went through the house looking for Jim but he wasn't there. The dark feeling of the dream lingered in her like a cold shadow she couldn't escape. She suddenly felt the urge to go see the fortune-teller again. Put on a shawl and left the house and walked up the street to where the old woman lived. There were potted flowers on the windowsill, and from the street, Luz could see a bird in a wicker cage just inside the woman's open window. It chirped as though crying for its freedom.

The fortune-teller said, "I was expecting you."

They went into the drawing room where a small round table, a deck of cards, and two chairs stood. There was nothing else in the room but an oval mirror. She sat across from the woman and waited, then remembered the price and took it out of her reticule—one dollar—and placed it on the table, and the fortune-teller stared at it for a long moment before picking it up and putting it inside her blouse.

She was as ancient and wrinkled as a biblical fig, her hair white as a virgin's soul. She had small, curious eyes that seemed to float in their sockets, a tiny little thing hardly larger than a twelve-year-old child.

"Give me your hands, dear."

Luz held forth her hands, and the woman took them in her own. The woman's hands felt like wax, the fingers with their long, yellowed nails curled round her wrists as though she were about to pull Luz from deep water.

The woman studied Luz's hands, reading the lines the way a cartographer reads a map he's just made. She began to hum lowly between pursed lips.

At last she released her grip and settled back as though having completed a long and exhausting journey through dry land. Sighed and closed her eyes.

Then: "That which you love will soon be lost to you."

"What does that mean exactly?"

The woman shook her head, opened her eyes. They were eyes that lacked any true and single color, the eyes of a ghost, Luz thought.

"I'm not sure," she said. "What is it you love?"

"My children and my . . ." She started to say, *My man*, but caught herself. Is that what Jim was, her man? She wasn't so sure, because even though he'd asked her to marry him and she had said yes, she was afraid there were things about him she didn't understand, things that made her fearful to give him all her trust without question. He was still a stranger to her in many ways, she realized after having watched him on the street with those two men, how he was ready to kill them both.

"Yes?" the woman said.

"There is this man . . ."

"It could be him . . . it could be one of your children."

"You can't tell me?"

"I can't. There is only so much I am able to see. Only so much light I can carry into the darker world."

"When will this happen?"

"Pretty soon. The aura around you is very strong, the lines in your hands broken."

Luz looked at the palms of her hands. But weren't all lines in people's hands broken?

She looked at the woman's hands. Her lines were not broken except for one place.

"I will pray for you, child," the woman said. "It is all I can do."

She smelled of dead flowers, and Luz left quickly in order to stand in fresh air again. She vowed she would spend no more time or money on the fortune-teller—that she was just some crazy old woman who kept herself alive on other people's fears and desires. Perhaps fear and desire were the same things—that what we most desired was what we most feared. She wanted love the most, to love and be loved again as she had been with Hector. But now that it had been offered to her in the form of another man, she was afraid to love so completely. She feared if she gave Jim all her love as she had done with Hector and something happened to him too, it would destroy her.

She went quickly to the jail hoping to find him, looking in the windows of the café as she went to see if he was in there eating.

She found him instead writing something there at the jail, sitting behind a desk. He looked up and put down the pen when she entered.

"You left this morning without saying anything," she said.

"I didn't want to wake you."

"Why not? You always have in the past."

"I knew you were upset with me."

"I had a bad dream."

"About what?"

"You and me and Hector."

"But it was just a dream."

"I went to see the fortune-teller."

"What did she tell you?"

"That I would soon lose that which I love."

"You believe her?"

"No."

But Jim could see the doubt in Luz's eyes, could feel it as palpable as the heartbeat in the wrist.

"Let's get married and leave this place," she said. It sounded to him like a question more than a request, something to test his love for her.

"Where would we go?"

"Anywhere . . . Texas. I have a brother in Texas who owns a big ranch. You could work there and we could live there. My children would love it."

"It's not a bad idea," he said.

"But?"

"I need to be my own man, Luz. I can't work for nobody but me."

"You're working for somebody now."

"Just for a real short time, just to get a little something put back into the bank. Then I'm back to horses. Horses is what I know, what I love doing." He paused, then added: "Horses and you and having a family. I never thought I'd want a family until I met you, Luz."

"You can get horses in Texas," she said.

"I like it here. I have my own place for the first

time in my life. I'm not going to let somebody run me off. You're worrying for no good reason."

Suddenly the prisoners began to yell.

"When the fuck we gone get something to eat!"

"Go on home, honey," he said. "I'll come round later. I don't want you subjected to this riffraff."

She threw her arms around his neck.

"Please," she said.

He held her a moment, then undid her arms and led her to the door.

"Go on home, honey."

And when she left, he went to the rear cell and stared at the two of them through the bars.

"You keep your mouth shut or I'm going to beat it shut."

"You plan on starving us to death?"

"Don't give me any new ideas," he said, and walked out.

Chapter Twenty-Four

Jim finished what it was he had been writing and folded it carefully and put it in his shirt pocket while he waited for Woody to come relieve him. He wanted to have a long conversation with Luz, explain better to her things about himself, things until now he'd assumed she would understand about him without his having to explain it. If she wanted to know everything, he decided, then he would tell her everything—the good and the bad of what his life had been till the day he met her. Wipe the slate clean and start fresh. It made sense.

Then Bucky Weaver's kid, Arturo, he believed the boy's name was, shuddered the door open and said, "I need help!"

"What is it?"

"My old man's killing my old lady . . ."

Jim knew the family slightly.

Bucky was a teamster with a good-size mouth on

him, especially when he got his drunk on. Liked to
fight with his fists, cuss anything and anybody who
looked at him cross-eyed. Jim figured a man like
that, it didn't matter if the one crossing their eyes
was a woman or not, was his own wife or not. Had a
brood of kids ran wild like prairie chickens, this one
included, who'd steal a damn rusted bottom bucket
or strips of barbed wire from fencing if nobody was
looking, they were so damn poor. The bottom of the
boy's bare legs were scratched and he was barefoot;
his clothes hung from him like dirty washrags.

"You sure they're not just arguing?" Jim said.

"He knocked her down and two teeth out of her
mouth." The boy opened a dirty hand, and Jim saw
something that tied a knot in his stomach: two pieces
of bloody bone that surely were human teeth.

He grabbed his hat on the way out the door, wishing Woody had come in, but he hadn't yet and there
was no time to go look for him if what the kid said
was true, and he didn't see how it couldn't be—a
man knocking his own wife's teeth out.

"He been drinking, your paw?"

"Yes sir, about all day."

"He knock your maw around a lot when he's like
that?"

"Some but nothing this bad."

The kid hopped aboard a twisted-ear mule and
punched his heels into its ribs hard as if he was trying to kick in a door locked from the inside. The
mule brayed and showed its teeth against the bit

but trotted off, and Jim mounted the stud and followed.

Far as he knew, Bucky Weaver kept a shack southeast a mile or two you could see from the road once you got close because of the big windmill Bucky had built and painted red for some goddamn odd reason.

Jim rode alongside the boy and said, "Your old man got many guns?"

"A few."

"Where's he keep them?"

"One by the front door and one in the bedroom."

The sun threw their shadows out in front of them.

"What started this thing between your maw and paw?"

"Nothing."

Jim hated a woman hitter as much as he hated anything. And it seemed like it was always the meanest and biggest sons of bitches that married the smallest women and did the hitting.

They rode on in silence, the kid kicking and urging his mule to go faster. They topped one rise then another, then saw the red-painted windmill clacking gentle in a soft but steady breeze.

Jim drew rein, said, "You best wait here, boy."

"But—"

Jim cut him off with a hard look.

"It could be bad down there, real bad."

Jim rode steady toward the house. It seemed quiet, peaceful, no shouts or bloody screams coming from it. Bad sign, Jim thought. He pulled his revolver and dismounted, keeping the stud between him and the front door. He glanced back to see the boy still sitting the mule, jug-eared and staring.

"Hello the house!"

No answer.

"Hello the house!"

There was a dreadful long silence, then: "What you want, mister?"

"Constable Glass from Domingo," Jim called. "Your boy summoned me, said you were having a bit of trouble out here."

"No goddamn trouble here. You might as well get on back to wherever the hell it is you come from."

"Like to talk to you a minute if I could."

"Got no time for jawing."

"Like to talk to your missus then."

"What for?"

"See if she's doing okay?"

"What the hell business is it of yours if she's okay or not?"

Jim noticed there weren't any of those wild kids running around. Chickens scratched in the yard, but not even a dog to bark and raise hell. He figured the other kids had run off too.

"Come on out here a minute," he called.

"Go to hell and get off my property while you're doing it."

"Can't."

"Why the hell can't you?"

"I'm the law is why."

"Shit, not around here you ain't."

"Afraid so. Law's the law, no matter."

"I'm gone come out there and bust your ass you don't get."

"Better come on then."

Jim waited until the door creaked open, and Bucky appeared in it holding a single-barrel big bore in both hands like an ax handle he was getting ready to split wood with.

"Best drop that piece," Jim said.

He could see Bucky trying to figure out how to make his move with Jim keeping the stud between them.

"Boy," the man called to the kid farther on. "I'm gone whip your ass for bringing the law to my door. You best climb down off that mule and get in here."

"He's not going to come in there, Bucky."

A guttural sound croaked from the man's throat.

"You know me?"

"I know you by reputation. Am told you're a mean drunk. Understand as how you like to knock women around. Now call your wife out here to me so I can have a look at her. She's okay, I'll get on my horse and ride out."

"I'm gone shoot your damn head off."

Jim didn't see a way around it. He rested the pistol steady on the seat of his saddle, aimed just where the man's legs forked, knowing the bullet would drop several inches, squeezed the trigger until the pistol banged like a door slammed shut. Bucky yipped and dropped his big bore and fell straight down. Jim crossed the yard before he could get off his ass again.

"You shot me in the goddamn leg!"

"You didn't give me much choice. I was aiming for your nuts."

Jim called the kid and told him to go and find a belt or a piece of rope and tie off the bleeding leg, reached and took the big bore and broke it open, saw there was a twelve-gauge shell in the breech, picked it out with his finger and thumbnail like a piece of walnut meat and dropped it in his pocket, then flung the gun out into the yard.

He went inside, and it looked like the whole house had been cyclone hit, furniture overturned, dishes broke, shelves busted loose from the walls, a window broke out. He found the woman huddled in a back room separated off from the other two rooms by a blanket hung from nails pounded into the jamb.

She was holding her face, and blood had dribbled out between her fingers and dried on the backs of her bony hands.

He knelt down beside her.

"You okay?"

She shook her head.

"Of course not," he said. "You want me to take a look?"

She shook her head again.

"How about I take you into town and have the doctor look at you?"

Again she shook her head.

"I'm going to arrest your old man for beating you."

"No!" she sputtered. He saw then where the two teeth had been, the split lips, puffy now, the right eye bulging dark as a plum.

"We need him here—to put food on the table . . ."

"Yes ma'am, I understand all about that, but you can't let him be beating on you this way."

"He won't do it again," the words coming out cluttered like she was chewing a piece of beef and trying to speak around it. Jim helped her stand and walked her into the main room where there was a pan of water atop a dry sink at one end, and he took a piece of frayed cloth hanging from a nail and dipped it in the water and wrung it out and touched it to the woman's battered mouth. She lifted her harried gaze, and he understood all there was about the hard times she'd gone through and hoped to God he'd never be in such a situation, and knowing more certainly he'd never put Luz or any other woman in a similar situation. He did his best to keep his anger tamped down for her benefit.

He went back outside, and Bucky was sitting there

moaning his pain, gripping his thigh where the bullet had gone in, a leather belt cinched now above his knee. Jim took out his Barlow and slit open the torn and bloody trouser leg and felt around back of the wound where there was another larger one and said, "My bullet went right on through, I doubt it broke so much as a bone, but it took a good-size chunk of meat out of you."

"Well, goddamn, ain't I the lucky one it didn't break no bone!"

Jim saw the boy standing there staring, told him to go and round up his siblings and get them back here to help his maw. Then when the boy ran off, Jim turned his attention back to Bucky.

"I reckon you are one lucky son of a bitch because I'm not going to beat you like you beat her. At least not right now even though I'd like nothing better. I'd haul your stupid ass to the jail and lock you up in it but for her pleading with me not to. But I will tell you this one thing: I ever come back out here because you hit her, and I'll bury you out back of beyond."

Bucky was on the verge of tears from the booze wearing off, the pain like fire in his leg crawling up into his groin, the realization he was faced down by a man in front of his own family—the worst possible indignity a man like him could suffer.

The boy came back, his siblings in tow, who all went into the house except the brave boy. Jim stood and walked him off a little ways from the house.

"I don't care what it takes, he ever hits your mother again, you come find me. You understand?"

Arturo nodded his head.

"Or if he ever hits you over this, you come and find me."

"Yes sir."

Then Jim walked away, took a deep breath and exhaled, wanted to swear, but didn't. Mounted the stud, started to ride away, then pulled up and said to Bucky:

"Heed my words."

The eyes of the two men met across the span of space, and both knew which had been licked and which hadn't, and who would be licked even worse the next time they met under similar circumstances.

Jim nodded, turned the horse out to the road and back to town, never realizing what he was about to ride into.

Chapter Twenty-Five

When Woody got to the jail the chair behind the desk was empty, but both prisoners were still in their cell much to his relief. *I sure don't hope I get fired over being late*, he thought, and sat down at the desk.

He had looked at the two of them locked up and they looked at him, and something shivered under his flesh and he thought: *The eyes of evil is what I am looking into*. Well, he knew he'd never make a career out of being a lawman, and perhaps it was time he more fully concentrated on what he knew he could be good at. He planned on sending off a batch of poems to a publisher in New York, soon as he got relieved of his duties this day. They were poems about his adventures thus far in the West, of Westerners, those plainspoken, often drunk and loud men, their profanity and tendency to engage in fights, their often lurking silences before they

exploded into violence. And speaking of explod-
ing into violence, could any of God's creatures be
more prone to such than a horse? He thought not.
He smiled at the thought and set the small elk-skin
satchel with his poems and his journal there on the
desk.

He took out his pen and his journal made of
heavy cardboard covers and pages of plain heavy
stock paper, his bottle of ink, extra nibs, and spread
them before him.

The events of the double killing had been nag-
ging his thoughts ever since he'd witnessed it, and
he thought he would write a poem about them as a
means to clear the emotional wreckage the shootings had rent. Though he didn't want to be overly
dark, he thought it his duty as an observer of his
times to pen what he'd witnessed in the terrible
murders of Trout Threadneedle and Tug Bailey.

> *In peaceful morning's yawn, who could*
> *Predict the coming storm? O' great peace*
> *Where did you flee this bloody morn?*

Well, it was a start, even if not a very good one.
It was always difficult to convey in lyrical form that
which is stark and painful as a broken bone.

He felt suddenly as lost as he'd ever been. What
was he doing in this place of such violence anyway?
It wasn't what he truly wanted. It wasn't Paris or
London, a place of peace and civility, a place where

the art of poetry was respected and appreciated. Here there were just horseshit and mud and men bent on killing one another over almost any perceived offense.

He immersed himself so completely in the poem that he barely felt the pistol's butt pressed into his lower ribs until it became physically painful, then took it out carefully and put it in the top desk drawer. Had decided in a moment that he would tell the constable upon his return that he was quitting, that this wasn't what he was cut out for. And instantly felt relieved at his decision. He would mail off his poems with a return address of Albany, New York—the stately old house of his parents, and move in with them until something broke for him even if he would have to work in his father's hardware store until that time when a publisher would recognize his talents.

It was such a sweet, pleasant thought until suddenly the door jumped open and two men stood there in the small space of a room with him, guns cocked and aimed—large revolvers.

"We come to post bail for them two you got in back," the one said. Woody had never seen either man before this moment, but he had no doubt these two were made of the very same stuff as the ones locked up in the cell. He swallowed, and it was as though he was trying to swallow a whole crab apple.

"Get them keys, boy."

"Yes, sir . . ."

But Woody did not move.

"I said get them keys!"

"I can't."

"Why can't you?"

"I swore an oath."

Hatch looked at Willis.

"You believe this stupid son of a bitch?"

Willis shook his head.

"No, I don't believe anybody can be that dumb."
Then to Woody, Willis said, "Are you that fucken
dumb?"

Woody knew the drawer he'd put his own pistol
in also contained the keys to the jail cell. Just inches
from his fingers. But could he do it? Or would he do
it? Therein lay the great question of all time, for all
men everywhere—could they, or would they?

"I'm going to paint the walls with your brains
you don't get them fucken keys and get 'em now,"
Hatch repeated.

Woody shook his head. His mind was telling him
one thing, but his body was in opposition.

Hatch shot him between the eyes. The poet seemed
to stare into another world, then fell forward, his
head slamming into the desktop, knocking over the
bottle of India ink so that ink and blood mixed together upon the poem's lines—black and red make
purple—and drowned the few lines of words as
surely as a burst dam would drown the people living below it.

"Dumb fucker," Hatch said as he searched the drawers for the keys and found them hooked to a big metal ring along with the pistol and walked them both to the back where the cell was.

"Well, we're into it now," Willis said.

"We didn't come here to twiddle our thumbs."

Cicero and the half-wit were standing at the bars, anxious, having heard the gunshot. They put big clown grins on their faces soon as they saw Hatch and Willis, Hatch carrying the key, putting it in the lock, turning it and swinging the door wide.

"Just posted you boys' bail," Hatch said. "You ready to go make some money?"

"Been ready since I was born," Cicero said. The half-wit stared at the dead deputy, the way his glasses had twisted off his face, the spreading pool of blood and ink.

"You're a killing son of a bitch, Hatch, just like me," the Mortician said.

"You can take credit for this one too, if you want," Hatch said. "Add to your reputation."

"Shit, I don't need no freebies, I got plenty as it is."

Outside Hatch said, "Where your horses?"

"Don't know, that son of bitch took 'em, I guess."

"So what's our play, now that we're all one big happy family again?"

Cicero told them about the bank.

"I thought maybe that was it when I seen it.

Didn't we think maybe that was it when we seen it, Willis?"

"We did," Willis said.

Pablo was mucking stalls when four men approached. He recognized two of them, the small one and the big one. Thought the new constable had 'em both locked up. Now here they were with two others wanting horses.

"Sí, I have your horses, señor. But there is the matter of feeding and keeping them. The constable said that I would be paid . . ."

This time it was Cicero's turn. He shot the Mexican through the chest.

"That payment enough?"

Black Bob had gotten out of bed that morning in spite of the pain from the horse kick. Soon as Woody came and went again, he began feeling the need to rise up and see his duty done.

"Don't be getting no ideas about getting out of bed," his wife warned soon as he tried.

"You got to help me sit up."

"That horse kicked in all your ribs, man. How you goin' do anythin'?"

"Got to do somethin'. Now help me up outta here."

Felt like two loads of bricks sitting on his chest when he tried to move, pain so deep it burned his breath.

"Why you want to fool with this bidness?" she

said. "Let them white men be to they own mis-
chief."

"Took me an oath. Man don't goin' to pay me to
lay up here in this bed."

"Man don't pay you to get yourself killed neither,
far as I know."

"Ain't plannin' on it."

"You don't know what you be plannin'."

"Help me put on my boots . . ."

"No sir, ain't goin' hep you do anythin'."

"Woman!"

They rode up the street and tied off in front of the
bank.

"You know how you want to do this?" Hatch
asked Cicero, who had his mother's eyes and nose,
and when he looked into those eyes, he saw the old
lady, there on her knees that day, looking up at him,
knowing she hated what he made her do for two
dollars, knowing he'd make her do it again if he
ever got the chance.

Cicero looked at his uncle.

"Bloody is how," he said.

"Fine by me. Willis, you and Ardell wait here
with the horses; we won't be long."

The two of them went in, guns drawn.

Hadley Prine was tying his shoe, bent over in his
chair behind his desk at the bank. Glen was waiting on a customer—Joe Toe, who sold supplies

for windmills and came through Domingo once a month to deposit his money. Nearly eighty dollars hard cash he didn't feature carrying around on his person.

The door crashed open, and it drew everybody's attention, and Joe Toe said, "Jesus Christ, it's a robbery!"

Hatch shot him where he stood. Cicero Pie shot Glen, a man who moments earlier was as giddy as a schoolgirl knowing he was going to go over to Polly Edwards's place that evening to have supper with her and maybe a lot more than just supper if it went good as it had the last time they'd had supper together. It was an event he'd been looking forward to all week.

It was not a completely clean and killing shot, and as Glen lay on the floor bleeding out, looking up at the stamped tin ceiling, he told himself over and over again that this was just some bad dream, that he'd wake up and Polly would be there smiling at him from the other side of the teller's window. That everything was going to be okay, even with the taste of warm blood choking him. And there too was a darkness creeping into him, a dark, indescribable feeling like a man might have if he was being chased by a bear, knowing he couldn't outrun it.

He heard their voices, those men who shot him and Joe Toe. Heard them shouting orders at Mr. Prine: "Get that goddamn safe open, you son of a bitch! Do it now!"

Glen felt himself slipping away into the darkness. Didn't want to go, couldn't stop it, couldn't do nothing but just let it happen. He clawed the floor trying to hold on, scrabbled his feet trying to keep from sliding off into the void.

"Good gawd! What is wrong with you men?" Hadley Prine wanted to know just before Hatch struck him across the face with the barrel of his pistol.

The cheekbone cracked like an eggshell and shot bolts of pain straight into the banker's skull like hot needles, causing him to reel like a drunk on a swaying ship's deck. He had to catch the corner of his handsome desk to keep from falling.

Cicero Pie stuck the muzzle of his pistol into the banker's face and said, "Your life worth all that money?"

The banker stumbled to the vault and began fumbling with the combination, but his mind was all jumbled. The gun pressed at the base of his skull wasn't helping any.

I knew I should have become a haberdasher like I wanted instead of listening to my father, he silently berated himself. *People don't rob haberdashers and shoot their assistants and customers . . .*

Chapter Twenty-Six

Hairy Legs, fresh from his liaison with the German's wife and hungry as a badger from all the energy he'd expended trying to satisfy her—no easy task to be sure, because her own hunger was like a wildfire roaring through dry timber—met the white man on the road to Domingo, the road from his place cutting to the main road at a right angle.

The breed thought it strange the man was coming from that direction and not the other where his place lay.

"You still looking for those horse killers?"

"Found 'em."

"That a badge you're wearing?"

"It is."

"What happen, the white devil decide to quit?"

"He's dead, made that way by the horse killers."

The breed blinked at the news.

"Stuff happens fast."

"Yes, I guess it does."

"Thought maybe you were still out looking for 'em," the breed said, looking back the direction Jim had come from.

"Had to go out to Bucky Weaver's and settle a family dispute."

"Bucky drunk again, raising hell?"

"He was. Using his wife pretty hard. His boy came and got me. Bucky knocked two of her teeth out."

"Bucky's a bad devil with liquor in him."

"Well, I told him if he did it again, I'd bury him."

Hairy Legs smiled a pleasant smile, part of it afterglow from his encounter with the German's wife, and partly because he wouldn't mind seeing Bucky Weaver put down in a grave. Bucky had tried to run him over once with a freight wagon when he was walking along minding his own business on this very road.

"What about you?" Jim said.

"Going to town. Hungry as a wolf. Eat some of that German's food."

"Thought you were going East, find that Free Love Society."

"Think I already found it."

"Oh?"

The old breed let a smile crawl across his mouth, a smile most inscrutable.

"Maybe I'll just save my money," he said.

They were a quarter mile out when they heard gunshots.

"Shit," Jim said, and spurred his horse forward at a gallop.

Hadley Prine waited for the bullet to come. Gritted his teeth preparing for it as he turned the last tumbler on the combination and jerked the handle that would open the big steel door. But instead something struck him a painful blow over the back of his head that caused him to stagger, then fall off his feet, swooning into a gray unorganized world as he fell.

He lay there pretending to be dead. Half wishing he was. Through his squinting eyes he looked directly into the staring ones of Glen. Noticed they were pale blue—the first time he'd ever noticed that particular feature of a man who'd worked for him going on ten years.

Oh Glen, he wanted to say. *I'm sorry. I'm so very sorry for never having paid you more attention, for never having asked you even once what it was you thought about, what dreams you had, or who your parents were or where you were born. I'm sorry I never got to know you better. I'm sorry.*

He heard the chink of coins being dropped, the crinkle of paper money being stuffed into bank bags, the labored breathing of men robbing the vault.

Let them have it, he thought bitterly. *Let them have every damn filthy dime!*

* * *

Jim reined in at the jail, was off his horse almost before it stopped. The sight of Woody, facedown in a pool of still wet and spreading blood and black ink, stopped him in his tracks. He knew before he went to the back that the prisoners were gone. So were the guns . . .

He came out again, the breed still sitting the horse, curious now as to what was happening.

Others had come out onto the streets when they heard the shooting, timidly they came, cautiously they came, curiously they came. Most of them were still gun-shy from the previous shootings, and nobody who'd witnessed the killings wanted to be themselves the victims of the next violence.

Jim swung his gaze up and down the street and saw two men in front of the bank astride horses holding the reins of two other horses and he knew what was happening—knew it as well as he ever knew anything.

He jerked the rifle from its scabbard and jacked the lever moving forward toward the pair in front of the bank, stopped a dozen yards short and took aim and hit the big one—the half-wit—the bullet twisting him in his saddle. He let out a yelp like a frightened child that had just been scalded by a hot stove.

The other man with him reined his horse around, a pistol already in his hand, and fired, clipping the dirt in front of Jim. Jim was already levering the

Henry again and firing, levering and firing until he knocked that man too out of his saddle.

But the big man turned his horse Jim's direction and kicked his heels, running the horse straight at him. Yelling, cussing, screaming.

Jim barely got the lever jacked again when the horse swiped him and knocked him spinning into the dirt, the rifle tumbling from his hands. The half-wit whipping the horse back around, trying his damnedest to run over the lawman. Jim rolled away, but the half-wit swung a fat fist down, striking Jim across the back of the head and knocking him into the dirt again.

Jim fumbled for his pistol, but it had fallen out of the holster of his shoulder rig. He saw it lying there in the street and went for it just as the half-wit ran his horse at him again. The force of it nearly knocked him cold, but he managed to grasp the Merwin Hulbert just before he got knocked down.

Then there was a blur—a flash of something— and Jim rolled onto his back in time to see the breed putting all his weight behind the blade in his hand, driving it into the horse's belly and ripping it lengthways, spilling the oddly colored grayish blue entrails as the animal's front legs buckled and the big man went tumbling headlong into the street.

"You ain't the only one knows how to kill a horse," Hairy Legs said to the half-wit as he struggled to gain his feet.

But before Ardell could get up, Jim shot him again; this time he made sure to hit him dead center, made sure to put him down permanent, and down he went.

Luz heard the gunfire and closed her eyes against the fear. She knew he would be in the middle of it—too many gunshots not to be. She ran out of the house without thinking anything other than she wanted to save him, to give her own life if she had to. She ran and she ran.

They'd come out of the bank firing their pistols. People cleared the street, windows broke, horses tied up at the rails broke loose and ran. One horse collapsed from bullets. Each of the two men carried a heavy canvas bank bag in one hand and a pistol in the other and more pistols stuck in the waistbands of their pants.

They saw immediately that Willis and Ardell were both down. Saw one man standing in the middle of the street, a gun in his hand: that fucking goddamn lawman! Cicero Pie felt a red-hot fury at the same moment that Hatch saw the breed holding the bloody knife.

"Kill them all!" he yelled.

Jim stood his ground even as the breed folded from a bullet.

Held his ground and took aim even as another bullet ripped through his side and another hit him

high in the leg. A rain of bullets it felt like. A with-
ering gunfire that no human being could expect to
survive given time to think about it.

But there was no time to think about it. There
was only time to act. And old instincts took over
and Jim Glass stood there firing at the pair of bank
robbers and they fired at him.

He was gone now, into that place where men like
him went in the face of danger, into that strange,
quiet place that doesn't allow room for self-doubt
or fear. Everything was slowed down. Everything
framed before him: the gunmen, the buildings, the
sidewalks, the dead horses in the street, the dead
men in the street, the patch of blue sky overhead. It
was his town, it was his problem, it was his life they
were trying to take.

Then a sudden explosion and then a second, like
the crash of thunder and God Almighty.

And the street was suddenly cleaned of the two
men, both blown away in a gray smoke cloud that
just seemed to hang there.

Jim looked round, saw Black Bob holding the
shotgun leaking smoke from both barrels.

Black Bob saying, "Jeez Christ," and clutching his
chest before sitting down on the edge of the boardwalk to catch his breath, the buck of the shotgun
almost like a second horse kick.

Jim saw Luz running toward him.

She was saying something, calling something to
him.

He saw again the bright blue sky overhead, then her face above his.

"Jim," she said. "Jim . . ."

He didn't know why she seemed so worried.

"It's all right," he said.

"Everything's all right."

The sky was as pretty as he'd ever seen it.

Chapter Twenty-Seven

"**I** still don't know why I ain't dead," Hairy Legs told the German's wife. "That bullet should have killed me but it didn't."

"I'm leaving my Hans," she said.

"Why?"

"I vant to live wid you."

He sat by the window and studied the streaks of rain as they coursed down the panes of glass as if he were studying a schoolbook he had to take a test on the next day.

"No good," he said.

Her jolly face crumpled.

"Without you, he will go out of business. I won't have no place to eat."

"I'll cook for you."

"Wouldn't be the same."

She wept. He went outside in the rain. It was a

lightly falling rain that speckled his old army jacket with dark spots and gathered in his hair. The bullet had struck one of the brass buttons that slowed it considerable, and it just ended up there under the skin where he easily dug it out with the tip of his knife, then fused the wound closed by heating the blade and cauterizing the wound. Hurt some, the burning worse than being shot. When it happened, he thought, *This is it*, and sat down right there in the street next to the dead half-wit and his deader horse.

And by the time he realized it wasn't nothing that was going to kill him, that everything was over, that everybody that was fated to be killed that day was, and the rest were among the living and would remain that way, he knew all he needed to.

A strange turn of events, he thought.

She came and stood in the doorway of his place— the river running muddy brown, cutting along its banks, cutting a new course each time so that the river was always changing, never in the same place.

"Please," she said.

He turned, the rain in his hair and running down his face so that the rain could easily have been mistaken for tears if somebody looking at him didn't know any different.

"I think I'm going to go East," he said.

"Oh!" she moaned and ran and got into her buggy, took the whip and lashed it over the rump of

the harnessed horse, sending it into a bolting trot.
He watched her ride off.

Once was enough, he thought. *What would I do
with a wife if I had one?*

Then he mounted the horse the man had given
him and rode to town and sat there while the funeral
procession formed out front of the undertaker's.
Several men carried a lone coffin into the waiting
hearse. Practically the whole town had turned out
and stood waiting in the rain for things to begin.

Bilk and Little Paris were there among them.

It was the second day of funerals.

The day before the town had buried Woody and
Glen, Pablo and Joe Toe; even though Joe Toe
wasn't one of their own, he'd died in the bank
doing business. And after Woody and Glen, Pablo
and Joe Toe, they buried the four outlaws—whose
identity remained mostly a mystery to them all except for two names written in the hotel's registry:
the Mortician and his Assistant.

They hired a dozen men to dig graves, and all the
dead were buried in the cemetery side by side by
side, for death held no prejudice and the good earth
cradled the sinner and saint alike, and a man got
paid the same to dig a grave for an outlaw as he
would digging a grave for a lawman.

"It's a proper day for a funeral," Bilk said. "This
rain."

"It is, ain't it?" Little Paris replied. "But gawd, it
is so sad."

"Maybe that's the last we'll see of such violence for some time. It feels like a storm that's just finally blown itself out."

"I doubt the peace will hold long," she said. "It never does in these parts."

"We can hope."

"We surely can do that. But soon as this is over, I'm leaving on tomorrow's train."

Bilk felt his heart sink.

"I will miss you like an arm cut off," he said.

"What a lovely thing to say. I was wondering if I could borrow five hundred dollars to get me started?" She never mentioned about the money she'd already saved, for a smart whore never talks about her life, she only listens to others talking about theirs—when they're in the mood to be talkative, and thank God most of the men she'd consorted with and who had paid her saw fit to be taciturn and kept their jaws locked.

"Yes, I suppose I could see my way clear to spot you a stake even though I wish you'd stay here with me," Bilk said.

"Consider it a loan," she said.

"I'll just consider it the price of falling in love," he said.

The Mexican musicians began to play and Alfred Burpee sat straight-backed atop his fancy hearse, and next to him his assistant, Melo.

"We been busier than two raccoons sucking eggs," Alfred said. "It pays the rent, but to be honest with you, I hope this is the last of it for a while."

Melo remained quiet. He had never seen so many dead bodies in such a short time. It was as though they were raining down from the sky. Men he knew and men he didn't.

"Might close up shop for a while and go to California," Burpee said offhandedly.

"See the ocean, dip my feet in . . ." It was something he'd been thinking about for a while and now that business had been good, he thought maybe he could afford the luxury.

"I might go see my people in Mexico, then," Melo said. "Take my wife and kids . . ."

"Good idea. A fellow can only take so much of this murderous business before he has to go do a little living."

"Sí."

She came proudly from her house wearing the new black dress. No veil for her. She wanted everyone to see her face, to see that she was strong, stronger than death, any death. She wanted them to look at her and know that she had loved this man—this Jim Glass, and not even death could steal that from her.

She had been with him in those last moments, had cradled his head in her lap and stroked his damp, warm face as he struggled to hold on.

"I wish . . . I wish . . ."

"What do you wish, my sweet?" she had said.

"I wish . . ." He struggled with it, and she kissed his eyes and lips.

"I wish we would have gotten married," he said finally, getting it all said.

She held her hand near his eyes, showed him the ring still a little large for her thin finger and said, "We are married. We always have been, *corazon.*"

He looked around at the other faces that formed a circle above him, the beautiful blue sky above them.

"I love you," he said.

As hard as she tried, she could not keep her tears from falling on his face; they did anyway. She started to brush them away, but he stopped her by taking her hand and holding it.

"Stay with me a little longer . . ."

"I will stay with you forever," she said.

"Yes . . . Just a little longer . . ."

Then she told him about the life she felt—the little spark of life she knew was growing inside her. But she could not know with any certainty if he heard about his son or not, for his eyes were closed, even though his breathing continued—just little sighs of breathing.

And now she came and they parted for her, these who had gathered to pay him respect. She arrived, and Bilk helped her into the buggy with Little Paris, and they rode together behind the hearse with the others falling in behind, folks in wagons and buggies, and men on horses. But this time the burial would not be in the cemetery, but on the ridge behind Jim's place—the one where he had buried his friends, the one he so often spoke of as being the most beautiful place he'd ever seen. From the ridge a man could look down on his holdings, the house that used to belong to Charlie Bowdre and his wife, upon the river that flowed eternally, upon the distant mountains that in the winter and spring held the purity of snow.

A freshly dug grave awaited; she would see that a stone was put in place, had already ordered it.

And when they made the ridge, the rain stopped as though commanded and the sky to the north cleared off clean as chalk erased from a blackboard, and while the priest spoke, she turned and saw off in the distance a small dark herd of horses grazing.

Wild horses, and thought, *They know, they have come home to be with him.*